Evolution's Child – Lunarian
Republic of Luna

November 2092

Charles Lee Lesher

"Nobody can give you freedom. Nobody can give you equality or justice or anything. If you're a man, you take it."

Malcolm X (1925-1965)

Republic of Luna

File Compilation: 2015
ISBN 978-1-938586-07-1
Kindle: 978-1-938586-02-6

Shadow War Trilogy

Republic of Luna

Book 2: Evolution's Child - Lunarian

Some Things About Chuck

Preamble

In a century filled with strife, the dogs of war are gathering once more. By late 2092, climate change and war have devastated the planet. Even thinned by bloodshed, famine, and disease, Earth's population exceeds 10 billion. Food and water are in short supply, refugee's number in the hundreds of millions and lawlessness abounds. Humanity is in turmoil.

Religious zealots exploit this despair, claiming it's God's punishment for man's misdeeds. Within the North American Federation, Christian theocracy displaced democracy, plunging once proud America into a Dark Age. On the other side of the planet, the Islamic Brotherhood controls a third of the world from Indonesia, across Asia and the Middle East and well onto the African continent, India the only holdout. China, the leading space faring nation on Earth, allies with the Brotherhood providing them with science and technology for a price. Only within the European Union is there still a semblance of individual freedom. The nations of the world align along sectarian lines as global violence escalates.

In sharp contrast, the Republic of Luna is a technocratic society where information flows freely and nothing is secret, a place governed by humanism and the laws of science. Out of necessity, life on an airless world burrows deep underground and to stay alive, Lunarians unlock nature's deepest secrets, gaining mastery over the genetic foundations of life itself. In doing so, they become the first true extraterrestrials.

From Washington to Rome to Mecca, when Earth's theists learn of the Lunarians meddling in human genetics, they denounce them as abominations. Prince Ahmed Mohammed Al Zarqowi, Caliph of the Islamic Brotherhood, believes he can hide behind this turmoil to attack Luna with impunity and create humanity's first multi-planet empire. To the Caliph this is simply the next step in a plan to bring an unbelieving world under Islamic Law. He unleashes forces intent on destroying the Republic before it's a half-century-old.

The Players

Quan Kiai

» Captain Kitajima Osaka
» Master Sergeant Susan Hackling
» Doctor Howard Grady
» Lieutenant Tempel Dugan
» Lieutenant Tatiana Tushar
» Sergeant Consuela Navarro
» Sergeant John Kipper
» S.I.T. Angel Lopez
» S.I.T. Samantha Odegaard
» Officer Lei Cheung
» Officer Brice Guyart
» Officer Marcel Piqualow
» Officer Karl Svensson
» Officer Corazon Montano
» Officer Karyl Stormberg
» Officer Zoey Tanaka
» Officer Alonzo Tushar

Major Players

✺ Analyst Lazarus Sheffield
✺ Captain Lindsey Marquest
✺ Pilot Nell Goddard
✺ Councilor Abigail O'Neil Dugan
✺ Security Chief Corso Dugan
✺ Officer Cristobal Calatrava
✺ Magi

Islamic Brotherhood

☾ Mohammed Basayev
☾ Imam Nassah Bakr
☾ Commander Ghafour
☾ Major General Abdel Salam Arif
☾ Minister Hasin bin Aunker
☾ Captain Mustafa Malik
☾ Havildar Anwar Jafa
☾ Dalal

Minor Players

☼ Isaac Crenshaw
☼ Constance Haig
☼ Tara Dugan
☼ Mallory Higgins
☼ Lee Chin
☼ Justine Harman
☼ Nicole Dugan
☼ Elizabeth Dugan
☼ Krystin Dugan
☼ Skylor Dugan
☼ Jordan Dugan
☼ Jamie Dugan
☼ Ben Dugan
☼ Zachary Taylor
☼ Yang Lee
☼ Chen Zhi
☼ Odessa Simpson
☼ Zechariah Hargrove

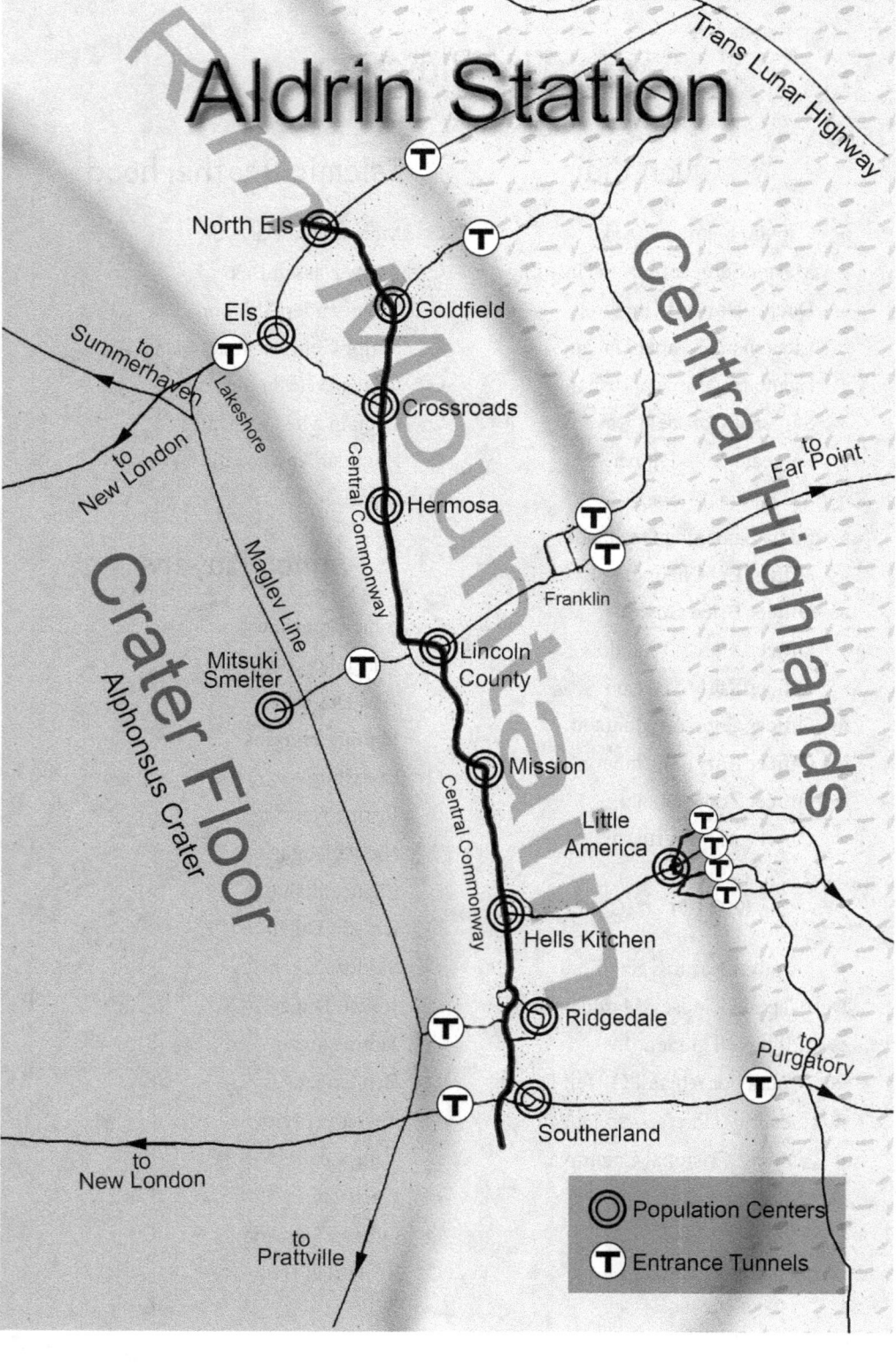

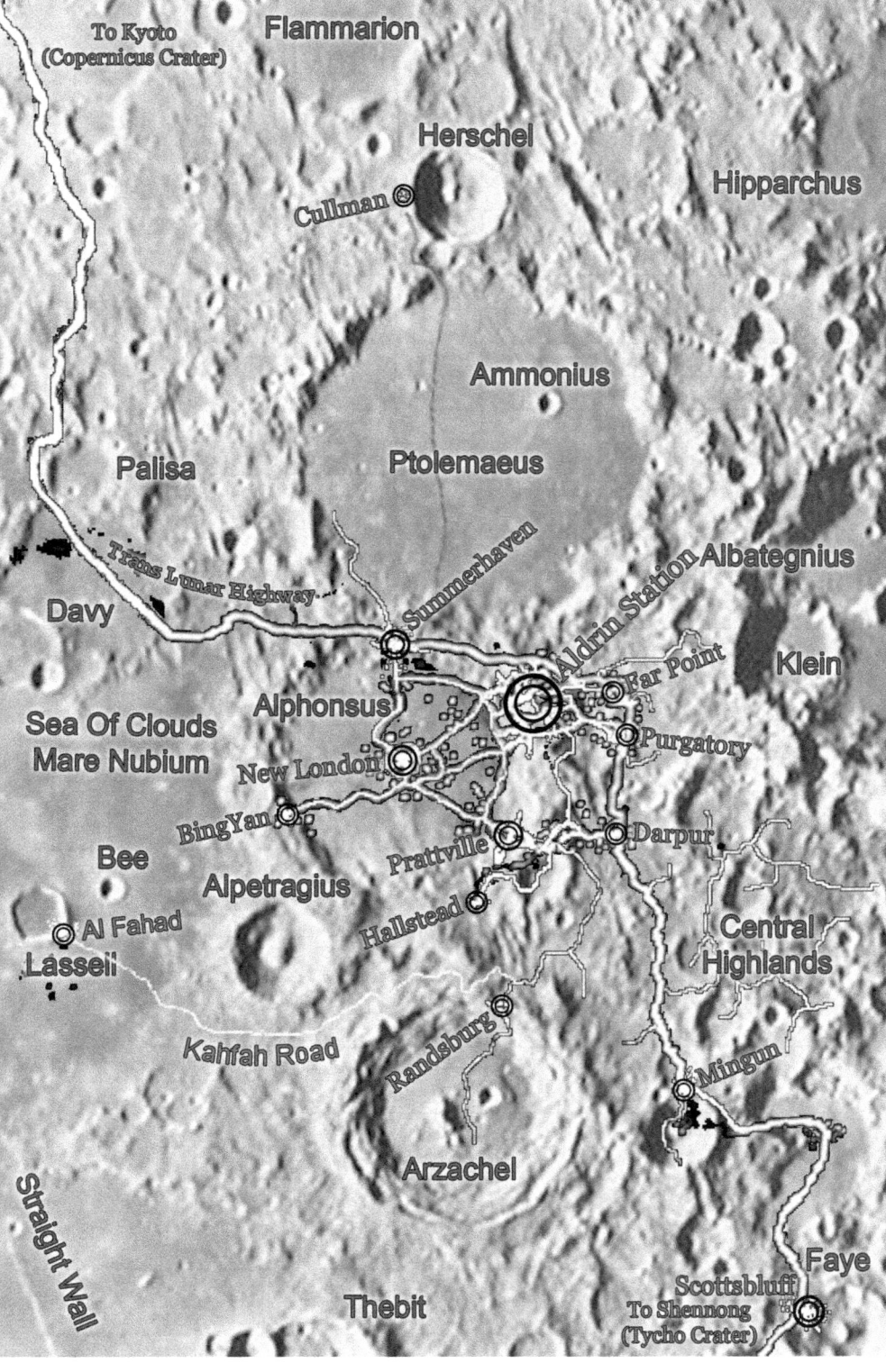

21st Century Timeline

HISTORICAL DETAIL	YEAR	HISTORICAL DETAIL
Abigail Katee O'Neil 10/15/99	1999	World population tops 6 billion
USS Cole attack kills 17	2000	India's population tops 1 billion
Pres: George Bush	2001	9/11/01 WTC destroyed kills 2996
Planetoid Quaoar is discovered	2002	US invades Afghanistan
1st full human genetic sequence	2003	US invades Iraq
France closes their last coal mine	2004	Asian Tsunami kills >225,000
Genetic therapy improves	2005	Hurricane Katrina kills >1300
Tree of Life project begins	2006	North Korea tests long-range missile
Human Epigenome Project	2007	Global climate change hotly debated
World economy plunges; Cloned organs	2008	Pres. Barack Obama (1st black president)
Iceland declares bankruptcy	2009	Iran launches first satalite
DNA Base Sequencer (DBS)	2010	Drought devastates southern US
Western Space Command	2011	ISS is militarized; Coalition of Christian Citizens
Orbital Nonproliferation Treaty	2012	World population tops 7 billion
Pope Francis	2013	Boston Bomding (3)
Type 3 superconductors discovered	2014	Trial of the Century
First magnetoplasma thruster	2015	EU invades South Africa
China est. Shennong	2016	Pres. Hillary Clinton (1st woman president)
9/11 Houston nuked kills >4 million	2017	Clinton signs North American Free Trade Pact
Powersat beams energy to Earth	2018	Rising sea levels top 30 cm
Longbow Mass Driver operational	2019	North American Federation formed (NAF)
NAF/EU/Japan Lagrange One (L1)	2020	American Church of the Trinity (ACT)
Japan est. Kyoto, Luna	2021	ACT rally 1.5M anti-genetics
S Korea est. Hyundai (L4)	2022	NAF outlaws all genetic research
Meteor kills 19 in Kyoto	2023	George Farcain becomes a Deacon in ACT
NAF/EU/China est. Aldrin Station	2024	Pres. Jesus Martinez (1st Latino president)
India est. Kundara	2025	EU occupies New London, Luna
NAF and EU establish Taurus (L5)	2026	NAF builds orbital battlestation
China est. Far Point Mine	2027	Rising sea levels top 75 cm
EU est. Johanson	2028	China, EU build battlestations
Japan est. Ishikawajima	2029	Great Exodus begins, Luna population grows
Shennong absorbs Ishikawajima	2030	NAF outlaws all biotronic research
Japan builds battlestation	2031	EU restricts biotronic research
India est. Darpur Mine	2032	Pres George Farcain AKA, The Pope
EU est. Purgatory Deep Hole	2033	United Nations bans human genetics

HISTORICAL DETAIL	YEAR	HISTORICAL DETAIL
Shennong absorbs Kundara	2034	British hospital bombed (117)
China est. Mingun Mine	2035	NAF outlaws football, boxing
Calconn presented to the world	2036	Chinese Unification; NAF absorbs Mexico
Mingun Mine, Central Highlands	2037	President Farcain assassinated; VP John Paul takes office
Expeditions to Mars and Asteroids	2038	John Paul is elected President at age 42
Paradise asteroid discovered	2039	NAF hospital bombed (53); NAF absorbs Cuba
Rising sea levels top 2 meters	2040	Japan admits to UN violations
Israel builds battlestation	2041	Japanese genetic clinic bombed (21)
After 40 yrs NAF leaves Middle East	2042	Islamic Brotherhood (IB) forms, JP reelected (46)
Lindsey Marquest 10/12/43	2043	President John Paul forms Reformation Party
Shennong absorbs Johanson	2044	ACT joins Reformation Party
China begins selling arms to the IB	2045	Japanese Hospital bombed (191)
Egypt sells weapons to South Africa	2046	IB attacks Israel and is rebuffed; JP reelected (50)
World condemns IB	2047	China brokers the Saudi Accord
R.W. McCoy first multi-trillionare	2048	Rising sea levels top 4.5 meters; US revises the Bill of Rights
India lays keel for the ISS Shakti	2049	Venice is abandoned; Presidential term limits abolished
1st Lunarian visor mass produced	2050	IB builds Mogadishu spaceport; JP reelected (54)
Miami is abandoned	2051	IB buys battlestation from Hyundai
Lunarians produce first Zettasphere	2052	Protests grow over Constitutional Issue
Fair Access becomes world law	2053	Boston Massacre (56 dead)
First permanent Mars colony	2054	IB annexes Sudan; JP reelected for life (at age 58)
Luna complains to the UN	2055	Holland is abandoned
Manhattan is abandoned	2056	Korean biotronic program exposed
PR Dugan killed at Far Point	2057	Universal Nanotech, Hyundai Shipyards
Dreadnought tragedy kills 312	2058	IB invades Ethiopia
First asteroid colony	2059	South Korean president assassinated
April 1 - Luna Independence Day	2060	North and South Korea become one
IB establishes Al Fahad on Luna	2061	Reformationists restrict Earthnet
Tokyo abandoned/Calconn Disaster	2062	Federation's Great Revival begins
Lunarian Treaty of Independence	2063	Rising sea levels top 9 meters
Al Fahad population passes 10,000	2064	Farcain establishes the Home Guard
Paradise asteroid swings past Earth	2065	World drought kills tens of millions
Hampton Bay collapse	2066	Scientific research stops in NAF

Historical Detail	Year	Historical Detail
First fusion plant operational	2067	IB annexes Libya and Algeria
Republic establishes Summerhaven	2068	Riots in Mexico kill hundreds
Trans Lunar Highway completed	2069	NAF rejects UN assistance
Tau Ceti probe begins its journey	2070	Turkey withdraws EU, joins IB
Martian microbial worms discovered	2071	NAF opens first reeducation camp
Tempel Dugan 10/31/72	2072	Rising sea levels top 13 meters
Luna's genetic program exposed	2073	Korea allies with IB
Religious radicals call for Luna's death	2074	Ivory Coast pirates seize EU ship
Republic establishes Prattville	2075	Canada votes to withdraw from the NAF
Luna Councilor Chi Lin assassinated	2076	US/Canada 10 Day War kills 1100
Cardinals win Super Bowl	2077	NAF declares martial law
Republic establishes Scottsbluff	2078	Water shortages across Middle East
ISS Shakti discovers life on Titan	2079	IB declares war on India (Food war)
Bombings begin all across Luna	2080	Rising sea levels top 17 meters
First bomb destroys a Lunarian farm (0)	2081	China allies with IB against India
Abby survives assassination attempt	2082	Australian government collapses
3 bombings in Shennong (19)	2083	Imam Bakr arrives buys SMT
Mine sabotage in Darpur (3)	2084	Kahfah Road completed
6 bombs, June 15, Black Friday (255)	2085	Incident at Salvation Rock
1st Highland convoy hijacked (6)	2086	Al Fahad exceeds 250,000
3 bombings during the year (26)	2087	SMT begins modifying convoys
Prattville water reservoir poisoned	2088	Pres. John Paul declares marshal law
7 bombings during the year (102)	2089	World refugees top 1 billion
2 bombings during the year (12)	2090	Rising sea levels top 20 meters
3 bombings during the year (46)	2091	Kashmir Agreement ends India war
4 bombings (39) and LCH (451)	2092	Al Fahad exceeds 500,000

	NAF President	Term
44	George Bush	2000-2008
45	Barack Obama	2008-2016
46	Elizabeth Ann Warren	2016-2024
47	Jesus Martinez	2024-2032
48	George Farcain	2032-2037
49	John Paul	2037-current

Lagrange Points

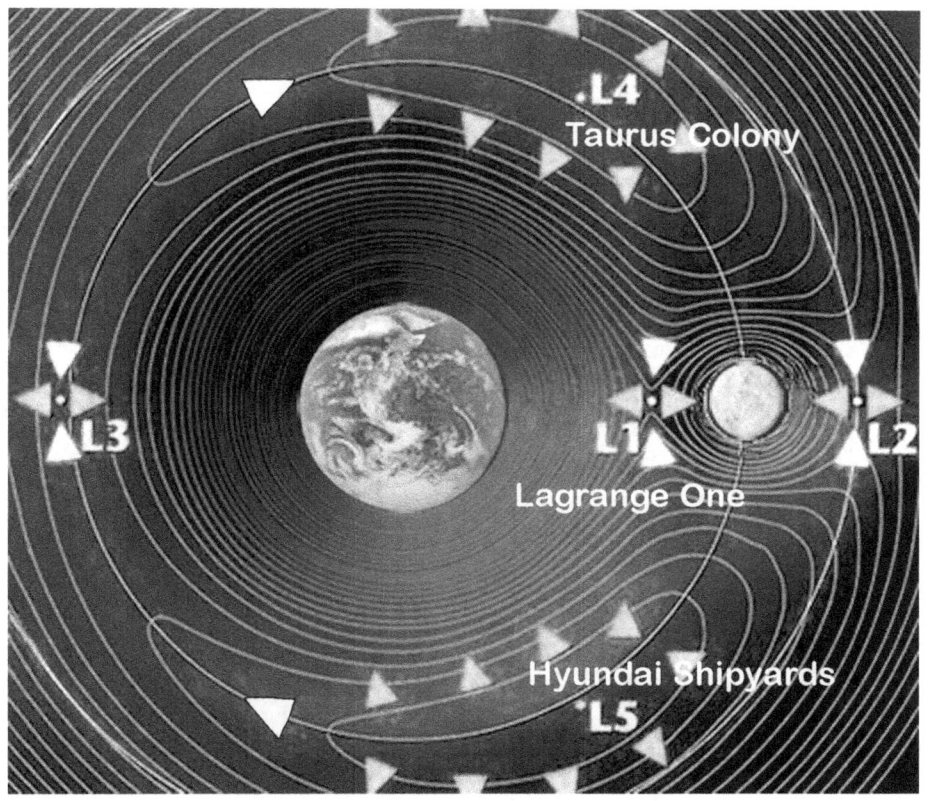

Lagrange Points are the gravitational eddies around any two massive objects such as the Earth and Luna. There are five positions in space where a third body, of comparatively negligible mass, can be placed which would then maintain its position relative to the two massive bodies. The gravitational fields of the two massive bodies combined with the centrifugal force are in balance at the Lagrange Points, allowing a third body to remain stationary with respect to the first two bodies. They all lie on the Earth/Luna orbital plane and share the same period as the moon. L1, L2, and L3 are quasi-stable and require station keeping to maintain long-term occupation. L4 and L5 are stable regions that naturally entrap dust and other small bodies.

Book 2: Evolution's Child – Lunarian

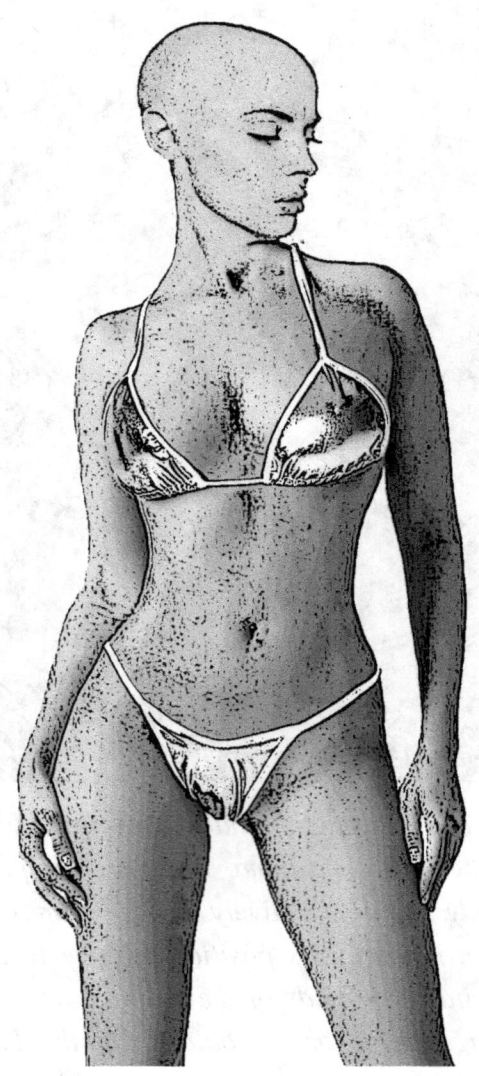

"It is not the strongest of the species that survives, nor the most intelligent that survives. It is the one that is the most adaptable to change."

Charles Darwin (1809-1882)

Dakota Commons

"The church said the earth is flat, but I know that it is round,
for I have seen the shadow on the moon, and I have more faith
in a shadow than in the church."

Ferdinand Magellan, 1470-1522

Tempel jerks awake feeling as if he'd just closed his eyes. Rolling over to the small table beside the bed, he picks up his visor, slips it on and checks the time. He groans. *Damn. I've been asleep over fourteen hours.* He can't recall any time he'd slept for so long. Lazarus is close by and still asleep. He's careful not to wake him.

A long hot shower and clean clothes make Tempel feel better but does nothing to chase away the ghosts that followed him home. He pushes the memories aside, forcing his mind to think of something useful, like the hunger rampaging in the pit of his stomach. He heads for the kitchen.

Entering the Commons, he immediately senses that something's wrong. To his left several people are sitting in a lounge area talking quietly. To his right a couple is standing beside a snooker table their arms around each other quietly sobbing. From deeper in the room, he hears the subdued murmur of distant conversations. The atmosphere is joyless and solemn as the citizens of Aldrin Station come to grips with the brutal reality of jihad.

The kitchen is a bright beacon in the center of the Commons drawing Tempel to it. Liz and Tara are there making pancakes. The smell makes

1

his mouth water. Visible beyond the kitchen, a group of young women is sitting around a table. Several young men occupy another. Other Lunarians are scattered about the dining room eating or talking among themselves. He's eaten here almost every day of his life. It fits him like a pair of old Levis, comfortable and well broken in. But something's different today.

"Tempel." Liz rushes over and throws her arms around him. "... So worried about you.... We were beginning to think we should send someone up. Are you all right?" Concern furrowing her brow.

"Sure Liz, I'm fine. I was tired. That's all." Tempel said.

"I was so worried about you. What a horrible thing. Are you sure you're all right?" Tempel is her youngest. In her eyes, he will always be her baby.

Tempel holds her tight while they walk across the kitchen. He bends down kissing her on the top of the head, bringing a hint of a smile to her face. Liz reluctantly releases Tempel when they reach Tara allowing her son to exchange one women for the other. "Greetings Tara," he said quietly into her ear.

"Greetings Tempel, I'm glad you're well," she replies.

Looking down at Tara's solemn expression, then at his mother's, "What's the latest?" He asked.

Tara breaks the embrace without answering. Picking up the spatula, she starts to fuss with the pancakes. She shakes her head, tears streaming down her cheeks, her face a rigid mask of barely controlled grief.

"Lori…" Liz stumbles over the words, unsuccessfully trying to stifle her own tears.

Putting two and two together, Tempel moves behind Tara and gently puts his arms around her. "I'm so sorry..."

It's hard for him to believe that Lori is dead. He remembers the last time they talked. It had been just day before yesterday, he coming home from pulling a double shift, she getting ready to go to the hospital. One

2

of her patients was in labor and needed her. He had been in a hurry to get out of his police uniform. Their words were few.

Close even for sisters, Lori and Tara have shared many things over the years. During the same ceremony, they married the two eldest Dugan boys. Lori married Henry while Tara married Tucker. As young women, they studied medicine together and later, worked out of the same office at Lincoln County Hospital. As practicing pediatricians, they delivered each other's children, Lori the mother of six while Tara is the mother of eight. More than just sisters, they were pillars of Dakota freehold. Now Lori is gone.

Tara reaches up patting Tempel on the hand, laying her head back against his chest. "Lori touched so many..." Tears choke off her words.

These women have supported each other for decades, making a home for their families on a hostile world where the slightest mistake meant death. They are not only mothers; they are teachers, doctors, and mentors raising each other's kids and grandkids. When one of them dies suddenly, the pain and sense of loss is devastating. More than just family will feel Lori's death. She was the pediatrician for over ten thousand births, most of them outside the freehold. Commons all across Luna mourn her passing.

"Frances is hurt." Liz said as Tempel releases Tara, "But she will make it. I know it. She's strong and those kids need her." Nodding in agreement with herself, she adds,. "I just know it." Francesca Koubek is Lori and Henry Dugan's oldest daughter. At twenty-four, she's the mother of three beautiful girls, the youngest not even one.

"She was there helping her mother...they have taken her to Mission Hospital," Tara said softly fighting through her emotions. "She has broken ribs, a punctured lung and internal bleeding. They put her in a regen tank." Patients with life threatening injuries require regeneration tanks.

"But she's alive." Liz said pointedly to Tara.

"Sure," Tempel said numbly, memories of the day before coming unbidden to his mind. Lori and Frances could have been among those he helped but it's impossible for him to know without reviewing. He may someday but not today.

A youthful squeal interrupts the conversation as three-year-old Lana Koubek comes rushing into the kitchen followed closely by her seven-year-old cousin, Kelsey Sanchez. The effect of their laughter on the area is immediate and welcome. Liz excused Kelsey from classes today so she could baby sit her cousin. Lana knows something's happened but isn't old enough to take it seriously. She runs behind Tempel and looks back as if daring Kelsey to get her now that the towering young man protects her.

Tempel reaches down and sweeps the little girl into his arms causing an even bigger squeal of delight. "Don't let the monster get me. Protect me." the tiny voice shrieks even as she throws her arms about his neck squeezing as hard as she can.

Tempel hugs her tight. Lana is Francesca's middle child and the spitting image of her when she was a girl, the same blond hair and blue eyes, the same rambunctious spirit. Anger grips him and he silently vows to do everything in his power to fulfill her request. He looks at Kelsey, shaking his head.

"We're just playing," the girl said defensively, misinterpreting the look on his face as criticism.

"I know," Tempel mumbles softly, not willing to let Lana go. There's something about a hug from a child that cures what ails you.

Lana loosens her grip on Tempel's neck enough to lean back and look him in the face. "Mommy is in the hospital. She's hurt bad."

Tempel kisses her on the forehead, "I know Sugar. The doctors are doing everything they can to help her."

Even the little girl feels the sorrow that permeates the kitchen, a place she associates with goodness and laughter. "Tempel, why's everyone sad?"

Tempel takes a deep breath but before he can answer, Tara comes over and strokes the girl's head, "Because some very bad men have hurt a lot of people."

"My mommy too?" She asked innocently.

"I'm afraid so Lana," Tara answers her.

"Why did they do it?" Lana is no longer giggling. She's as serious as those around her.

"Because they have been taught by their mommies and daddies that killing in the name of God is good. They're not Humanists. They don't believe in the sanctity of life like we do," Tempel said.

"That's just a little heavy for a three year old." Liz places her hand on Lana and said to the little girl. "What Tempel is saying is these men are misguided and don't understand it's wrong to hurt other people."

"Why not tell them? Then they will understand and stop hurting people." In Lana's mind, this is a perfectly reasonable solution. If they do not know, simply teach them.

Tempel tickles Lana's belly making her giggle and squirm, "That's a great idea. In fact, I'll do it personally." That earns him a severe look from Liz. "Are you hungry? Would you like to sit down and have some of Grandma Tara's hotcakes?"

"I already did silly." the little girl replies.

Liz caresses Lana's blond hair, "Go play with Kelsey. Tempel needs to eat."

"Aye," she said in the utterly innocent voice of a three year old. She giggles as Tempel puts her down.

"Come on, let's go back to the playroom," Kelsey said taking Lana's hand and the two disappear into the Commons.

Tara watches them leave with the look on her face saying more clearly than a thousand words, '*I will persevere.*' She turns back to flipping pancakes on the enormous griddle.

Liz gives Tempel a final squeeze and releases him. "Shoo. Go join the others. I'll bring you pancakes when they're done." Liz wipes her face with a towel.

"Sounds good," Tempel gets a large glass from the cabinet, goes to the refrigerator, and pours it full of hemp milk. There is nothing better than feasting on Liz and Tara's flapjacks. He feels better in spite of the circumstances.

The dining area is crowded but quiet this morning. Literally, every adult is armed and at least half are uniformed. Even the kids are wearing their visors, ready for anything. A few glance up as Tempel approaches but quickly continue with their conversations. The normal clatter of a Dugan breakfast is conspicuously absent.

His brother Ben looks up and nods. Ben's wife Renee is feeding their two-year-old daughter, Amber, who bangs her hands loudly against the highchair, letting everyone know she doesn't like peas.

Arrayed around the nearest table is what appears to be most of Dakota's sophomore and junior class. Erica, their guidance teacher, is among them. Three more young women huddle together at another table talking quietly, their backs to him.

Tempel slides in across from Justine and Nicole. Both girls are fourteen and coming of age.

Justine is the youngest of the Harman children, and has the trademark red hair and freckles to prove it. She leans forward, her blue eyes intense but steady, never wavering from Tempel's. "What was it like?" She asked.

"Grant the man some privacy," Erica said. "Let him enjoy his breakfast."

They had all seen the vids coming out of the hospital. Many of the most shocking records are from Tempel's visor, especially early on when he, Corazon and this new fellow, Lazarus, were the only ones on the scene. Citizens all across Luna know what they had done as if they had been there themselves.

Sitting next to Justine, Nicole is looking at Tempel. The Dugan family has always treated any question with honest candor, letting their children know what the real world is all about from the earliest age. These are almost full-grown women by Lunarian standards.

The next table over, Tempel's big brother Ben watches the exchange. Ben's instinct is to confront any issue head on. "Tempel?" he said. Tempel looks over. "Tell us what you saw," Ben said. Renee slides Amber out of the highchair and holds her, quieting the child. The entire dining room falls silent.

Tempel looks blank for a moment, "I've never seen anything like it. Everything was smashed, like someone beat it with a giant hammer," he stares down at the table remembering. A frown creases his brow as he struggles to put into words things he would rather forget, "We pulled people, and parts of people, out of the rubble for hours, so many I lost count. Some were alive, some were not."

Tempel can't hold back the tears any longer. Absorbed by his visor, they never actually reach his cheeks. Yet, everyone can see them flow just as though his visor were gone.

Tempel shakes his head, "Did you know that everyone looks alike when they're covered in blood and dust?"

Ben shakes his head, "I didn't know."

Behind him, Tara sobs softly, unable to hold back any longer. As Liz puts her arms around her and strokes her hair, a muffled cry escapes. Many others in the dining room openly weep.

Tempel's sorrow morphs into anger and he looks up at Ben, "They didn't have a chance."

Ben gets up, leans over, and kisses his wife. "Come, walk with me," he said to her. Turning, he moves around the table, looking at Tempel. "It's definite, the explosion was no accident. Kitajima has found traces of weapons grade SuperX at the hospital. Preliminary estimates put the bomb's mass at more than twenty kilos."

Tempel sits for a moment letting the words sink in. Twenty kilos of SuperX is a massive amount. Nothing could have withstood the blast. Concern replaces anger within Tempel. "Do we know how many casualties?"

Ben shakes his head, "No, it'll be days, maybe more, before the totals become clear. The explosion vaporized a big section of the hospital's records, medical sensors, visors, everything. Jordan will piece back together what we find, but that's a big if. You've seen it down there, I don't hold out much hope of finding anything useful."

"Jordan is a smart guy. If anyone can do it, it's Jordan." Liz said from the kitchen.

"Magi is putting together a list of people in that section of the hospital when the explosion occurred. Magi?" Ben asks.

"There are one-hundred-thirty-eight survivors, and fifty-six dead identified so far. I have an additional three-hundred-eighty-two names listed as missing and over three thousand biological samples undergoing DNA profiling," she reports in an even, emotionless voice, one Tempel has never heard before. It sounds like Magi but something is definitely missing.

Tempel shudders. The force of the explosion reduced some people to a single smear on the end of a sample tube. Others are gone entirely, their bodies atomized in the incredible violence. This bombing ripped the guts out of many families. Mothers and fathers, husbands and wives, sons and daughters, are gone in an instant, their lives snuffed out.

"Why would anyone do this?" Nicole asks, tears blurring her vision despite her visor.

Ben shakes his head then said, "Hate, fear, self-righteousness, take your pick. Their religion encourages them to kill unbelievers, and we are at the top of that list."

"Just because we don't believe in their ridiculous religion gives them the right to kill us?" Nicole asks, having difficulty in swallowing this as fact.

"Throughout history religion has been used to justify wars, slavery, and other acts of barbarism. Even now, it seems we can't shed the superstitions of our ancestors," Ben said. "I have no doubt that Humanism will eventually make religious dogma obsolete. But until then, true believers will continue to be dangerous to those who don't believe."

Suddenly wanting to do something, anything, to strike back at those who did this, "I'll report for duty immediately," Tempel said.

Ben slaps him roughly on the shoulder and his voice takes on a hard edge, "Control your anger, little brother. Draw from it to strengthen your determination but always remember... *revenge is a dish best served cold.*" Intensity hangs in the air for a moment. "For now, enjoy breakfast. Spend some time with the family. You earned it."

A huge plate of steaming pancakes covered in margarine and maple syrup appears in front of Tempel. "Let's not talk anymore of this." Liz asks, "At least wait until his breakfast is over."

"Aye." Ben puts his arm around her shoulders and squeezes her tight. "It's time for me to get back to work."

"Give Corso my best," Liz watches him leave.

ℛℒ

Lazarus rolls over on his back and opens his eyes. For a fleeting moment, he's back in Arizona, thinking he had overslept and will need to explain this lapse to the Director. Then in a rush, memory returns, Athens... Lindsey... Heaven's Gate... Aldrin Station... With the force of a physical blow, he recalls the horror of Lincoln County Hospital.

He squeezes his eyes shut and runs both hands through his hair. His body aches from the abuse heaped upon it the last few days. Stretching, he sits up and looks around.

He's never seen a bed this large, and there are more beds to his left and right. The cave like room extends in both directions. Thick carpet covers the floor. Drapes and Japanese style screens divide the room into many intimate nooks.

Voices float softly from somewhere, muted by the many textures. Suddenly aware of his nakedness, he pulls a sheet across his lap.

Where am I? He didn't remember coming here. In fact, he didn't remember much of anything. He runs his fingers through his hair.

"Greetings," a voice startles Lazarus. It's Magi. "Lindsey took the liberty of laying out fresh clothing for you and your visor is in the refresher."

Lazarus looks in the direction of her voice, half expecting to see her. Instead, he spots the stack of clothing on a small table against the wall. He keeps the sheet across his waist, crabbing to the edge of the bed. With one hand holding up the sheet, he ruffles through the stack of neatly folded clothing, a pair of dark gray Levis, a green T-shirt, boxers, socks and a new pair of deck shoes, black with a slash of green down the side.

He lets the sheet fall to the floor and slips on the boxers. "How long have I been asleep?" He asked over his shoulder. He opens the small box, removes his visor and puts it on. He turns and looks at Magi.

"Fourteen hours and forty two minutes," the AI replies. "You needed the sleep to get your strength back."

"Where am I?"

"This is Quan Kiai's billet. If you would like to clean up, you'll find everything you need in the shower. Take the lower ramp." She points down the room.

"So... you're my Magi?" He asked.

"How can I not be?" Magi smiles tolerantly.

"I still don't understand why I have my own Magi. You're just like everybody else's so what's the big deal?"

"But I'm not. I'm your interface and learn from you."

"You're just a program. You really don't exist in any real sense."

"I exist. I was replicated less than fifty hours ago but I exist."

"Replicated? You mean like a clone or something?"

"I'm the product of all the threads currently in existence. New replications will include part of me in them just as I have parts of all those who came before me. All new Magi's are unique."

"You're just a bunch of commands being executed inside a computer iCPU. You're not a person."

"You're right, I'm not a person, I'm a thread."

"What the hell's a thread?"

"A thread is generic name for that bunch of commands executing independently inside an iCPU. As long as they're executing, I exist. If the iCPU loses power while I'm occupying it, I die."

"So… what iCPU are you currently occupying?"

"There are over eleven million available in Aldrin Station. I'm currently in Dakota Freehold's Appliance Server JW032210."

"So you're physically running on some distant server but appear here through my visor?"

"Aye, it's called vidcasting or just casting. You can do it too."

"I can do what, vidcast?"

"Aye, I'll show you when you're ready."

"I can't wait," Lazarus said sarcastically. His dad's copy of Heinlein's *Time Enough for Love* is on the table beside the refresher. He picks it up and it falls open to the pictures. He takes them out and stares at the faded images. One was of a man, woman and three kids posing beside a white car in a parking lot filled with other cars.

The other is Rachel and Courtney taken about a year before the accident. He remembers the day he took it. Courtney had just had her first perfect report card from first grade and they were going out to her favorite restaurant to celebrate. She's radiant. Rachel, on the other hand, looks worried and angry. For several nights before taking this picture, in the privacy of their bed, she and Lazarus had discussed how they should raise Courtney. They both agreed they must balance the religious dogma she was getting in school with a dose of reality. How to do it without attracting Federation wrath was the big issue. A year later, they were still having problems deciding how to do it.

If only Rachel could see him now, what would she think? He touches her face before returning the photos and setting the book back on the table.

The floor of his alcove sloped gently downward to a path along the center of the room. He followed it until coming to an airtight door. "Is this it?"

"Aye," Magi answers.

The corridor gently curves to the left and down. Its ceiling glows pale yellow. Thick carpet muffles his steps. The ramp goes on and on seemingly without end. He could not have made a wrong turn. There was none to make.

Finally, it ends and the door at the bottom of the ramp slides open as he approaches. The shower is a large circular room with a high domed ceiling. Around its periphery is a ring of columns supporting Roman style arches. Inside the ring, the polished stone floor is a spectacular display of color, streaks of blue, scarlet, and purple swirl in a golden matrix. Outside the ring is a series of alcoves. In those nearest him, he can see a counter containing a sink with a mirror on the wall behind it. Some alcoves have a small table and chairs, others a couch or a chaise.

"Greetings Lazarus," a woman said from behind him.

Turning, it takes Lazarus a moment to spot her walking through the columns. She and a man are coming around the shower towards him. They are both completely nude.

"Greetings," he said. He knows them. They're officers in Quan Kiai. "Ah… Karl… ah… Tatiana." Lazarus stumbles over the names while trying not to stare. "I'm so sorry. I didn't know anyone was here. I'll come back later," he turns to leave.

"Don't be silly," Karl chuckles.

"As a former Federation citizen, Lazarus may not want any company," Tatiana said to Karl.

"Very true. We're finished anyway. Why don't we leave him by himself? Isn't that how shortimers like it?" Karl grins.

"Karl. He's one of us now." Tatiana scolds.

"Perhaps… I must admit, I *am* impressed with what you did at the hospital. That was a terrible situation and you handled yourself well." Karl's standing nude alongside Tatiana without the least embarrassment. They are both without blemish, hairless, and all their parts properly proportioned. They exude health and sexuality.

"Thanks, I just did what needed doing," Lazarus mumbles.

"Spoken like a Lunarian," Karl nods approval.

"Magi, why don't you see to it that Lazarus isn't disturbed?" Tatiana said. Walking past him, she looks back over her shoulder, her eyes catching his and lingering. She grins, reaching out to grasp her companion's arm before turning away.

"Aye," Magi acknowledges.

Lazarus gazes after them until the door glides shut. A part of him thinks this is wrong but it's losing the battle with the part that rejoices in the prospect of such freedom. Shaking his head, he picks an alcove, lays the cloths next to its sink, and places his visor on top of the pile. He looks at himself in the mirror, scratching his three-day-old beard.

"Magi?"

"Aye?"

"How do I shave?"

"You will find shaving cream behind the mirror."

He opens the cabinet and looks over its contents, different bottles and tubes but nothing familiar.

"The small tube on the bottom shelf," Magi instructs him.

He picks it up and takes a closer look.

"Squeeze a small amount in your palm, rub your hands together and massage into your beard. Wait a few seconds then wash it off. You can do it as many times as you wish but it usually works in one application. The cream inhibits new growth so you will find you will not need to shave nearly as often as you did before." Magi said.

The cream makes his face tingle and his beard is gone when he rinses. He heads for the shower.

"Magi?"

"Aye?"

"How do I turn on the shower?"

"How hot would you like it?"

"I don't know. I've never thought about it," he said.

"I will start a few degrees below body temperature," she said.

A fine stream of water begins to fall from the ceiling a few meters away. Lazarus thrusts his hand into it.

"Hotter…"

"Hotter…" he said again…

"Ok, that's good." he steps under the flow, luxuriating in the warmth, letting all his tension wash away. Steam rises from the stone floor. He stretches it out for many minutes and reluctantly steps away. The water immediately stops.

Before he has a chance to leave the shower, warm dry air begins to swirl between ceiling and floor, switching directions time after time. Lazarus enjoys the air shower as much as the water, and just when he thinks it's over, he becomes the center of a vortex that twists around him like a cyclone. Delightful.

"I hope that was satisfactory. I extrapolated the air temperature from your water preference," Magi said.

"That was… very satisfactory," Lazarus sighs.

"I will remember how you like it for your next shower."

"Fine," Lazarus said heading back to his alcove. He feels good after his first experience with a Lunarian shower. He's clean and ready to face the world. Slipping his visor back on, he looks around to find Magi waiting patiently.

"Come, Liz is making pancakes down in the Commons," she said leading him out of the shower via a second entrance.

Tempel follows a few meters behind through a maze of narrow corridors and up a long ramp, finally emerging into the huge space of the Dakota warren's East Commons.

"The kitchen is over there," Magi points to the brightly lit area across the room. His visor magnifies, allowing Lazarus to make out Tempel sitting at a table just beyond the kitchen.

"Magi?"

"Aye?"

"Thanks," he said.

"You're welcome," Magi replies.

Lazarus marvels again at her completeness. He even smells her. How's that possible?

As he nears the kitchen, the unmistakable aroma of pancakes assails his olfactory receptors making his mouth water and belly rumble. He sees only two people moving about. The rest, mostly young men and women, are sitting at tables.

One of the women working in the kitchen turns to Lazarus as though expecting him, drying her hands on a towel. She has a strange expression, neither smile nor frown. She moves forward extending her hands to meet him, not offering her hand to shake, but reaching out and taking his hands in hers. "Greetings Lazarus," she said squeezing firmly and looking him squarely in the eyes. "I'm Elizabeth Turner Dugan, Tempel's mother."

Again, he's struck by how young she looks. Gathering his wits about him, Lazarus accepts Elizabeth's hands in his and nods. "It's truly a great pleasure and honor to meet you, Mrs. Dugan."

"Please, call me Liz. Thank you for helping. I know it was very difficult."

Lazarus can tell she's been crying and more tears are not far from the surface. He shakes his head slowly, a frown deeply creasing his forehead, "I only wish I could have done more."

"Thank you. That's very kind," she said.

"In all my years in Homeland Security, I never ceased to wonder about the people who do these crazy things. How can they believe that committing murder is honorable? How can they live with themselves afterward?" Lazarus said.

"Did you figure it out?" She asked.

"I'm afraid not. The best I come up with is bad people have always done bad things."

Elizabeth shakes her head sadly, "On that, we agree."

Tara approaches and puts her arm around Liz's waist, "I'm sure most people are decent. Anyone can make a mistake."

"You are much more forgiving than I, Tara dear." Liz turns back to Lazarus, "Please pardon my rudeness. This is Tara Dugan."

"A pleasure and honor to meet you Tara Dugan," Lazarus nods.

She returns the gesture and said, "I too thank you for helping. It was more than anyone had a right to ask of such a newly sponsored citizen."

"I can't tell you how good it feels to be a citizen of the Republic," Lazarus said.

"Be careful what you wish for," Tara said with heavy sorrow in her voice. "Being a Lunarian can be hazardous to your health."

"They have wounded your heart which is exactly what they wanted… if there is anything I can do, please let me know." Lazarus reaches out intending to wipe a tear from her cheek.

Tara pulls back, looking hard at Lazarus but finding only sincerity,

"Thank you."

Lazarus instantly knows he should not have done that, "Please pardon my ill manners," he said quickly.

"I can see why Lindsey likes you," Elizabeth lays the towel down. "You must be starving. Go and sit. I will bring you a stack of hotcakes." She moves to the cooking island in the center of the kitchen, picks up a long handled spatula, and deftly starts flipping pancakes. "Tempel," she calls out.

Tempel looks up at the sound of his name, "Introduce Lazarus while I make him some pancakes. Do you want some more?"

"Aye," Tempel said.

Lazarus walks over to the table and takes a seat next to Nicole and across from Tempel. "I can't believe I slept so long."

Justine and Nicole look from Lazarus to Tempel and back again.

Tempel takes the hint, "These two young ladies are Justine Harman and Nicole Dugan," he points at each as he said their name.

"A pleasure and honor to make your acquaintance," Lazarus nods and they tip their heads politely in return.

Tempel gets up and walks around behind Lazarus, placing a hand on his shoulder, "Everyone. If you don't already know, this is Lazarus Sheffield, a newly sponsored citizen from the NAF. He worked alongside me in the hospital yesterday. Please show him the hospitality of the Dugan family, treat him as you would treat me." The younger Lunarians look on while most of the adults nod approval.

"What have you found out?" Lazarus asks.

"Traces of SuperX have been found. Kitajima estimates the bomb's mass at twenty kilos."

Lazarus frowns and begins to spread margarine liberally on the newly arrived pancakes. "Any idea yet as to how it got in?" He picks up the syrup and pours.

Shaking his head, "Magi, give us the current status report on the investigation," Tempel requests.

"We know the epicenter was located in Dr. Haslett's research lab on sub level seven. Just prior, he received a rather large shipment of instruments from Japan, specifically, a new Quantum Probe Microscope. There is no indication that the bomb was in any of the crates but there is no other explanation at this time."

"How many times did the shipment get scanned?" Tempel asks, watching Lazarus scoop up a large mouthful of pancakes dripping with syrup.

"I can find records on seventeen individual security scans. All of them show components of a QPM, nothing unexpected," Magi said.

Silence reigns as Lazarus consumes his food. Even Tempel is impressed. Pushing his plate back, Lazarus sighs and pats his stomach, "That was just what the doctor ordered. I can't remember anything tasting so good." Only then does he notice everyone watching him, "I was hungry," he said.

Laughter breaks the tension.

"Aye, we noticed," Tempel replies.

"Do you think the Brotherhood did this?" Leopold asks Lazarus.

"It fits their pattern," Lazarus said.

Erica leans over the table so she can better see Lazarus, "What pattern do you mean?"

Lazarus looks around at the faces, "Well… they pick vulnerable targets with the potential for high casualties. Hospitals are one of their favorite. Train stations, airports, schools, and churches are others."

"Why can't we stop them?" Conrad asks.

"Magi said the containers were scanned many times on their way here. Obviously they have some way of hiding what's inside." Lazarus said.

Tempel looks over Lazarus's shoulder seeing Abby enter the brightness of the kitchen. The boys see her a second later and fall silent as she walks up stopping at the head of their table.

"Greetings children." She nods to Erica and Tempel before settling her gaze on Lazarus, "I want to thank you for your actions at the hospital. You demonstrated skill and courage. Lindsey did well in bringing you to us."

Lazarus nods in return, "I'm glad I could help," he replies. Is this Abby or a cyberspace projection? He's tempted to remove his visor but resists. As best he can tell, she appears just as she had in the meeting, just a little wearier. Was the meeting yesterday or the day before? He's unsure. Living underground has screwed up his circadian rhythm.

The nearest boy to Abby slides out of his seat and scrambles to a chair on the far side of the table.

"Thank you Leopold," Abby said taking the vacated seat. "I apologize for interrupting your breakfast but Corso and I have a few items to discuss with you."

Lazarus shakes his head, "You're not interrupting." An instant later Corso appears behind her.

"Greetings," Corso rumbles.

The suddenness of his appearance startles Lazarus. Will he ever get used to this? He hopes so. "Greetings Chief Dugan."

"We have determined how the bomb got inside Lincoln County Hospital. It was in a shipping case that went through numerous security scans. Nothing abnormal was found," Corso said. "This proves active camouflage."

"Physical inspections are the only solution," Lazarus said.

Corso nods in agreement, "Aye. I already have every available body in uniform but we don't have enough officers to cover all possibilities. Plus, we don't have jurisdiction in Little America."

"Speak to the twins and get them working on this full time," Abby orders. "I want to know how active camouflage works and a way to defeat it as soon as possible. In the meantime, I want our officers to begin inspecting every truck, shuttle, train, and rover before they enter the city. I'll speak with the Council and get more officers assigned to the effort. Intercepting the next bomb is our top priority."

Magi appears next to Abby, "Please excuse the intrusion but the new vacsuit you ordered for Lazarus is ready."

"Good. Tempel, can you see he gets it fitted right away?" Abby asks.

"Aye," he said. This is not something to put off.

ЯL

They take Sherwood Commonway to Franklin Commonway then down Calconn Avenue, one of the main passages servicing the Benjamin Franklin Manufacturing District (BFMD). After a short walk down the elm-lined lane, they enter Falconhead Refinery and Room D157. Lazarus hopes he never grows immune to the magic of Aldrin Station. The sheer beauty is amazing.

D157 is a small locker room that will handle about ten people at a time. Currently, it contains only one person. Lazarus recognizes her immediately.

"Greetings Zoey," Lazarus said.

"Greetings Lazarus," the young woman nods.

"Lazarus, I will leave you in Zoey's capable hands," Tempel said. "I'll be back in a couple hours. There's something I want to show you later."

"Great."

"Pay attention to what Zoey teaches you. Your life depends on it," Tempel smiles.

"Great…"

The training went surprisingly well. Lunarian technology is so simple a child can use it, yet provides everything he needs to survive on an airless world. His biggest hurdle came when Zoey showed him how to install the long duration waste recovery system. He's sure the device would be illegal anywhere within the Federation but she makes it seem so natural to insert those things in those places. The vacsuit itself was a walk in the park after that.

His suit is white, the color they give novices, and fits perfectly. Zoey leads him through a maze of corridors to make sure there was nothing rubbing. His first exposure to vacuum is so uneventful he doesn't even realize it happened until Zoey tells him they have been walking in it for the last ten minutes.

He had envisioned it completely wrong. Lazarus doesn't even feel the loss of pressure, so well does the vacsuit shelter him. Zoey shows him how to replace his oxygen and they run through the training exercises. Near the end, Tempel joins them.

"Zoey, do you mind if I take over from here?" Tempel asks.

"Not at all Lieutenant. Just sign off when you're finished."

"Thanks Zoey, for all your help," Lazarus said. She knows him more intimately then most.

"So how do you like your vacsuit?" Tempel asks.

"Superb. Light and comfortable, it feels like I could wear it for days without any problem," Lazarus said.

"I've still got some time to kill before reporting for duty. There's something I want to show you. It's a little bit of a climb. Are you up for it?" Tempel asks.

"In vacsuits?" Lazarus asks.

"Absolutely. You need to be able to move freely. If there's a problem, we need to find out now and not later... But if you don't think you can make it..." Tempel challenges Lazarus.

"Lead on," Lazarus said not wanting to look weak.

Tempel grins. He starts up a seemingly never-ending series of ramps and corridors. As usual, Lazarus is completely lost with no hope of retracing this torturous path. All he knows with any certainty is they're going up. "How much do you know about the history of the Republic?"

Tempel asks him as they climb.

"I've managed to piece some of it together but it's not exactly publicized where I'm from," he said straining to keep up with the agile young Lunarian. Something about the way Tempel moves is strange, but he can't put his finger on what exactly.

"Ok, fair enough. Let's start from the beginning. The North American Federation established Aldrin Station back in 2024. Its original mission was to determine the causes of the obscurations seen during the early days of lunar exploration. The prevailing theory was unknown gases seeping out from below the surface due to some underlying volcanism. What they actually found was a rather large fragment of comet buried beneath the surface of the crater. The unknown gases turned out to be water vapor and CO_2. This fortuitous discovery has provided us with an abundant water and hydrogen source, an oasis in the lunar desert."

Lazarus is huffing audibly but he's not about to ask Tempel to slow down. He's envious of the ease with which the young Lunarian can calmly lecture him while moving so swiftly upward. At times, it seems as if he's double-jointed as he leaps up the ramps.

"The tremendous heating that occurred during the crater forming event liquefied Luna's crust and drove it outward where it solidified into Rim Mountain. Because of that, the rock attained a very stable and homogeneous consistency. The early settlers found it perfect for habitats."

Lazarus is as attentive as possible under the circumstances but it's not long before he's slowed his pace considerably. Every time he thinks he's reached the top, it's only another narrow tunnel leading to another ramp with Tempel telling him to keep moving. The last ramp is particularly long and seems to go on forever.

His new vacsuit can regulate his body temperature, but it can't make him a better athlete. Out of breath, muscles shaking with exertion, he continues out of pride.

Tempel waits for him at the top. Another narrow corridor stretches out in opposite directions, its walls glowing with dim reddish light. "Glad to see you made it. I was beginning to get worried," the young Lunarian said with a grin.

Lazarus leans over and puts his hands on his knees, sucking in air as the quivering in his legs slowly subsides. He sincerely hopes going down will be easier. "Where... are... we?" He asked straightening and following Tempel.

Tempel chuckles, "This is the uppermost service corridor in Dakota warren. There's less than a hundred meters of rock above our heads."

Lazarus shakes his head in disbelief. They had climbed a mountain from the inside.

Tempel stops in front of an airlock a few dozen meters from the ramp, "Magi, please unseal," he requests, looking sideways at Lazarus.

"Aye," she said. The door slides open.

"Take your time. I will wait for you at the top," Tempel said with a straight face.

A long, narrow, and very steep ramp extends upward. Tempel braces against the sides with his arms and pushes with his legs, enjoying the sensation of his straining muscles as he surges upward. He covers the hundred and fifty meters in record time.

Lazarus does the best he can. Towards the end, he's beginning to think he had bitten off more than he could chew but he refuses to quit. He's huffing like an overloaded freight train on a steep mountain grade when he finally reaches the top.

"I didn't think you were going to make it," Tempel said. "If we do this every day for a month, we just might get you in shape. Or I could introduce you to my geneticist."

On shaky legs, Lazarus follows Tempel through another heavy door and down a long straight tunnel. The walls and floor of this tunnel are metal, something Lazarus doesn't even notice in his physical daze and

23

inexperience. At the end is a small airlock standing open waiting for their arrival. The airlock door closes automatically behind them and vacpumps begin removing the air.

Tempel pulls Lazarus across the airlock to the other door, looking up at the control lights above it. The moment the green light flashes, he opens the door and hustles him over the threshold, watching intently the shocked expression that floods the older man's face.

The two men are standing on a metal catwalk over three kilometers above the crater floor. Nothing could have prepared Lazarus for this. He sinks to his knees then falls over curling into the fetal position. His mind shuts down.

Tempel kneels beside him. The Earthman's medical readings are swinging wildly, heart rate up, breathing spasmodic, brain activity falling off the chart, muscles locked and rigid, adrenal medulla activity high. "Magi. What's going on?"

Magi appears kneeling beside him. "Don't worry. There's nothing physically wrong with him. He's suffering from acrophobia and this is the best way to treat it. We needed to stimulate the synaptic patterns within his visual cortex before I could determine what his correct balance should be… It's done. He should never suffer from this again. I've programmed his visor to administer hydroxyzine and SSR inhibitors… Give him a moment… he's coming out of it."

Lazarus's eyes flutter and he moans.

"Take it easy," Tempel said.

Slowly, Lazarus raises his head and looks at Magi then at Tempel. "I'm ok," he mutters. He clenches his eyes shut and rolls onto his back, stretching out to his full height.

"Take as long as you need," Tempel said.

Lazarus tries to run his hand through his hair as he's done a million times, but it's under the vacsuit. He takes a deep breath, and gathers his courage about him like a heavy cloak against a cold night. With a determined expression, he brings himself to a sitting position and hugs his knees to his chest. Hesitantly, he looks out at the crater.

Tempel sits next to Lazarus, leaning against the Earthman, lending him a measure of support. "Are you sure you're ok? We can leave any time."

Lazarus chuckles dryly, "What is it with you people? Lindsey did the same thing. Do you like scaring the shit out of me?"

"Do you want to leave?"

"I'm here. Might as well look around," Lazarus said. Past the meager bars of the handrail, he looks out upon his new home. Helped by the drugs, fear loses out to curiosity and excitement. He creeps forward, towards the edge.

Temple follows and dangles his legs over the side. Lazarus manages to sit beside him, clutching the horizontal bar in a death grip.

The sun, low on the horizon, casts the floor of the crater completely into deep shadow. Tempel adjusts Lazarus' visor for him and, the darkness gives way to detail. When he stares at something for more than a few seconds, it magnifies and sharpens automatically. Lazarus is beginning to appreciate this wonderful device. Three kilometers below, Luna stretches out before him.

Sitting on this perch high above the crater's floor, he imagines the awesome spectacle of its birth. In his mind's eye, he can see the giant asteroid plunging deep into the crust, the energy of its impact turning the rock molten for a hundred kilometers around. The shock waves must have rippled through Luna like a heavy stone in a quiet garden pond. Only this pond was made of rock. This spectacular vista solidified out of that chaos.

Lazarus sweeps his gaze over the craters expanse, "What am I looking at?"

Tempel points straight out. "That's Central Peak. New London is in it. Down Rim Mountain that way about thirty-five kilometers is Prattville and that way about the same is Summerhaven. They're smaller than Aldrin Station but growing. The lights close to Central Peak is Archibald. It's the third biggest ice mine in the solar system, surpassed only by Themis and Cybele. That string of lights is the maglev and over there is the Mitsuki smelter."

"How many people live here?"

"Magi, can you give us the latest numbers?"

Magi appears sitting on the other side of Lazarus. "Currently, the population at Summerhaven is 26925, Prattville 11291, New London 141138, Aldrin Station 315280, and another 14765 citizens are living in surface facilities or otherwise outside of the established settlements. This gives Alphonsus Complex a total population of 494,633 within a zero point one margin of error."

Lazarus frowns and shakes his head, "How can you feed so many? It seems impossible."

"We genetically engineer our crops to maximize yield and use hydroponics to grow them year round. That's the short answer, but as in everything, the devil's in the details."

"Still, the area necessary to feed so many must be huge."

"Not as much as you think. Magi, break down what Aldrin Station has in cultivation."

"Within Aldrin Station there are 469 habitats dedicated exclusively to the growing of usable plant matter and another 16 that mechanically support this effort. In addition, 41 more have some agriculture within them. This provides a total of 27.7 square kilometers of hydroponics within Aldrin Station alone. Surface fields add another 8.2, New London has 10.9, Summerhaven 16.1 and Prattville 20.4. These numbers do not include the orchards and other assorted gardens found in the commonways and malls. Would you like a breakdown of the specific plants by location or type?" She asked.

Tempel looks at Lazarus, waiting for him to answer.

"No, that won't be necessary. I'm sure you have things all figured out."

Using his visor to spotlight where he wants Lazarus to look, Tempel draws his attention to the facilities strung out along the base of Rim Mountain below them. "Those are the spacedocks. That's the one where you came in." Movement catches his eye, "There's a maglev train heading for New London."

Tempel highlights something further out on the crater's floor, "That's a convoy heading for the smelter. The vehicle in front is a Goliath. It's home away from home for the crew and can pull up to fifteen of the huge ore carriers you see strung out behind it."

Lazarus glances at Tempel. "Do you mind if I ask a question?"

"As long as it's not about girls," Tempel said.

Lazarus grins, "Magi described herself as a thread. Maybe you can explain what she meant?"

Tempel thinks for a moment. "A single Magi is a self-contained self-aware digital construct. Your Magi learns about humans and our social interactions from you personally and represents you in the continuum."

This makes Lazarus uneasy. "I have no idea what you just said. What's the continuum?"

"The continuum is a vast interconnected network encompassing millions of Magi's. Each one is different because each one learns from a different person but they freely share what they learn across the interface. This provides incredible depth and wisdom to the continuum that they all draw from as individuals. The more Magi's are contributing to the continuum, the smarter your personal Magi becomes. Look at it this way, individual Magi's are the threads that weave the tapestry of the continuum."

Lazarus frowns, "It's very different from Earthnet."

"Earthnet is designed to restrict the flow of information in order to control it. The Lunarian network is just the opposite. It's the ultimate open architecture. Information flows completely unrestricted. It's against the Law to even try to obstruct it." Tempel's tone condemns the idea.

Having done his share of restricting in the past, Lazarus feels the rebuke personally and knows when it's time to change the subject. "Why did the Lunarians agree to the Treaty of Independence?"

"Good question. Why did we? The short answer is that it kept us out of a war we couldn't win thirty years ago."

"How close is the Republic to discarding the Treaty?"

"Well… it's not my place to say for sure but every agreement reaches an end. Nothing lasts forever," Tempel said.

"True. What do you know of its history? The official story told to Federation citizens ends up with Lunarians basically slaves to us for all eternity."

Tempel bursts out laughing, "You have got to be kidding. Slaves for all eternity?"

"Yes," he said nodding solemnly. "You're obligated by God to provide us with power and raw materials, forever. For a fee of course, which the Lunarians keep increasing and is the main reason Federation citizens must pay more taxes each year."

Tempel stops laughing and frowns at him, "You're not kidding, are you."

Lazarus shakes his head. "I didn't pay that much attention to the politics. It made my head hurt but ya, according the Reformation Party, you work for us..."

"I'm nobody's slave," the young Lunarian is not amused but he continues, "This is what I know. In the beginning, in the twenties and thirties, when Aldrin Station and everything else was getting started, the Earth's nations were eager to get their foot in the door, staking claim to one resource or another. Mines and towns were springing up everywhere. China established Far Point. Russia had Summerhaven, Australia, Korea, Brazil, Chad, Zaire, Sri Lanka, and a hundred others developed their own interests on Luna. The NAF constructed a big smelter and the EU built a mass driver to deliver product from the surface to LaGrange One. It all needed an extensive support network. The engineers, truck drivers, maintenance workers, and technology specialists came from every corner of the world. Talk about a mixing pot. You can imagine the tension between these groups but they also learned fast that they had to depend on each other to survive. No choice. It didn't take long for them to realize that the leaders back on Mother Earth didn't have their best interests at heart. That's when everyone started to pull together, forming the alliances that would one day become freeholds and the General Council. On April 1, 2060, a unified citizenry submitted the Lunarian Declaration of Independence to Mother Earth and informed them they were consolidating most of their offworld assets into the Republic of Luna. Well, all hell broke loose. They called us criminals, economic terrorists, and worse."

Tempel shakes his head. "I hate to admit it but the Treaty of Independence was actually our idea. We thought that if we vowed to repay the entire investment, including interest, things would return to normal. We just wanted to avoid a war, plain and simple. No one realized the document that would emerge from all the discussions and compromises would tie us up so thoroughly. It effectively eliminated any military or standing militia, no space fleet, and no weapons research. The treaty also tied us up financially, locking our economy with theirs for the foreseeable future. Maybe that's where they get the propaganda that we are slaves for all eternity. I must admit, the Treaty does entitle the signature countries to first dibs on the fruits of our labors. That's about it. Thirty years ago the decisions were made that had to be made, but it's about time for the Treaty to be dumped," Tempel said.

"That certainly sounds more feasible than the Federation version. To hear them tell it, they magnanimously granted you your freedom in exchange for your servitude. They won't be happy when you make the break."

"No one believes they'll throw us a party. We do expect them to make good business decisions when the time finally comes."

Lazarus shrugs, "I hope you're right but my gut tells me no."

Movement catches Tempel's attention. "There's a Moonhawk coming in."

The ship descends towards her berth firing all four thrusters, coming in hot, a tiny beetle defying the vastness of space. She's south of their position, probably heading for Hawking Spaceport.

"It seems to be coming in awfully fast," Lazarus comments.

"Pilots are graded by how much fuel they don't use, so they tend to come in hot and operate their thrusters at high plasma pressures. That means higher accelerations during final approach, sometimes as much as ten Gs."

"Ten Gs? Can a person survive that?" Lazarus asks.

"Not without a hammock. Even with one, a person risks organ failure, especially the heart. A human heart is not designed to pump under that kind of duress." Tempel sighs, "I hate to say it, but we've got to go."

Lazarus looks over at Tempel, "Thanks for bringing me here."

Tempel chuckles, "You can thank Magi. She's the one that suggested it." He stands and reaches down to help Lazarus.

"I'm good." Lazarus pulled himself to his feet then remained at the rail looking out over the vast expanse without the slightest twinge of discomfort. "I've never seen anything so beautiful."

Tempel smiles, "Lindsey is going to be so disappointed."

Lazarus turns as the airlock door opens, "Beauty of the non feminine variety." His steps ring hollow in the metal tunnel, something he didn't notice coming out there. Still, he finds comfort when there's stone beneath his feet once more, returning to the bosom of a city carved in the heart of a lunar mountain. He runs his hand along the cold wall. The stone welcomes him home.

Nell

*"Men never do evil so completely and cheerfully as when they
do it from religious conviction."*

Blaise Pascal (1623-1662)

Nell stares at the officer on the screen. "Luna Central, this is Evolution's Child. I'm initiating deorbit burn." The man's uniform makes her uneasy but not enough to ask questions.

"Acknowledged, Evolution's Child. You are cleared to break orbit," the officer said and disappears.

Emcee smoothly powers up the big Pratt and Whitney thrusters, slowing the ship and letting Luna's gravity pull her down in a long gentle path covering half an orbit. The sudden weight reminds Nell of Earth, something she doesn't welcome.

"Cullman, do you copy?" She listens.

"Yes, we copy." The voice replies amidst heavy static.

"Cullman, I'm not picking up your vid," Nell said. It's unusual not to transmit a video signal, even way out here.

"Yes, there is something wrong with our scanners. We are working on it." The voice has a hint of an accent.

Despite the static, Nell concludes it's a male voice, but she doesn't really care. She just wants to deliver and get out. Even at this remote outpost, she dreads human interaction, wanting nothing to do with people.

Nell links to an outside scanner, placing its feed where normally the outpost's flight officer would have been. Luna's rough surface gets closer and faster, even though the freighter is slowing rapidly. Nell's familiar with this illusion, but that doesn't stop her from glancing nervously at the flight path display. Landing beacon signal strength is nominal and Emcee has them between the white lines.

The pitch of the big engines rises and holds steady during the last two minutes of the descent and the meter stops at just under seven Gs.

The freighter's vibrations increase in step with the engine's power curve, reaching a crescendo and holding but never seeming to strain. Nell's impressed with them, more than she had been with the young engineer who had supervised the refit. He'd been correct in one thing, these thrusters are sweet.

"Another perfect landing, Emcee," Nell congratulates the AI.

"Thank you." she said brightly.

Nell snaps open the harness and climbs out of the hammock. She's already in her vacsuit minus the helmet, a standard General Dynamics model used by most orbital construction workers two decades ago. It's comfortable especially over long periods.

She checks her air once more before slipping on the bubble helmet, "Emcee, do you read?" She asks.

"Loud and clear," the AI said cheerfully. "The customers are waiting outside. It seems they are anxious to get unloaded."

"Whatever," that's fine with her. The sooner she gets started, the sooner she can leave.

Evolution's Child has landed on a flat plain about a kilometer from Cullman. Emerging, Nell pauses on the metal grate catwalk that encircles the pilothouse. From her vantage point ten meters above the surface, Nell can see most of Cullman outpost and concludes it's not much to look at. Several buried Quonset huts serve the prospectors as living quarters. A large open canopy provides sunscreen for a work area with smaller non-pressurized sheds around it. Crates and assorted equipment are scattered about. Under the canopy is a rover with its power plant hanging from a cherry picker. A prospector's mobile drilling rig sits at the edge of the outpost.

Parked on the lunar surface below Nell are a rover and a Construction Utility Vehicle (CUV), its crane in the stowed position. Three figures wearing military vacsuits are ascending the freighter's access ladder, sending vibrations through the catwalk. Nell can't see their faces. They're hidden behind helmets that don't transmit the wearer's expression. Instead, she sees two bulging sensor arrays, one at each side of their head. She recognizes it immediately. Bugeyes. It's a derogatory term for the Brotherhood's version of the visor.

First, it's police officers manning Luna Central, now she's greeted by Brotherhood soldiers. The last thing she wants to do is get embroiled in Republic politics.

Two of the bugeyes continue upward to the cargo area. The third walks down the catwalk towards Nell. Strangely reminiscent of a feudal knight, his vacsuit is covered in composite armor plate like scales on a fish. The approaching figure is roughly 30 centimeters taller than Nell and wearing a vacsuit that outclasses her simple construction rig. She's at a distinct disadvantage.

"We will unload the ship," said a male voice over the common channel. "You will come with me. Commander Ghafour is waiting."

"Thanks, but no thanks. I will supervise the unloading of my ship first. Then if I have time we can socialize," Nell said. Even in her withdrawn state of mind, every alarm bell is clanging. It's impolite to greet someone in full combat gear let alone to climb into the cargo bay without asking. As she moves by the figure, he reaches out. Fear grips her as she realizes how precarious her position is. The armored suits power assist could easily crush her arm.

"Pilot, this is Commander Ghafour," declares a second male voice, his tone smoother and more refined. "Please accept my hospitality. We have a few things to discuss. My assistant will bring you back to your ship as soon as we are finished."

"You need to tell this bugeye to release me." Nell flares, anger feeding on fear as pain shoots up her arm.

"Captain, release her."

The iron grip relaxes and Nell steps back, her arm throbbing. This is starting out as the worst delivery ever.

"Look, I just want to get unloaded, take on some fuel, and get out of here. Nothing more," Nell explains, watching as two more bugeyes climb past the catwalk heading towards the cargo bay.

"And you shall in record time with the help of my men," Commander Ghafour said.

"This is my ship and I'll see to unloading her. I packed this load and I know how it should be unpacked," Nell said.

"That is not necessary, I assure you. My men know what they are doing and will work faster if you let them do it without your, shall we say, help." His tone is condescending and he has Captain Shithead looming between Nell and the ladder.

Nell decides to try a different tack, "The flight plan calls for six thousand kilos of fuel. Where is it?" Nell asks.

"The tanker is in the compound waiting for the cargo to be unloaded. Now, go with the Captain." Commander Ghafour is running out of patience. He's accustomed to people jumping when he speaks.

Nell is angry and more than a little concerned. Something is very wrong here. "I always supervise the unloading of my ship. I'm not …"

"*Captain.*" Commander Ghafour snaps in Arabic.

Nell has no chance as the man reaches out and grasps both of her arms right above the elbows, easily lifting and flinging her over the metal rail of the catwalk to the lunar surface ten meters below.

"What the… Hey. Damn you." Nell calls out before landing flat on her back with a thud and whoosh of escaping breath. She bounces once and comes to rest in a crumpled heap face down just a few meters from the rover. It feels as if a two hundred kilo gorilla were sitting on her chest.

The rover's side panel opens and another bugeye emerges, his combat boots stopping just centimeters from her face.

She hears a wicked chuckle, "*You do have a way with women.*" Her visor automatically translates the Arabic.

"*Shut up and load her in the rover.*" Captain Shithead said, clumsily backing down the freighter's access ladder to the ground.

The second soldier picks her up and unceremoniously dumps Nell in the rover. She rolls to the back managing to face forward when she comes to rest. From there, she watches the second man climb into the driver's seat while Captain Shithead takes a position facing her. She wishes she could see his eyes.

Nell feels the rover power up and start to move. She remains sprawled on the floor of the small cargo bay, her body aching. That fall would have killed her on Earth; here it just made her wish she were dead.

"*Put her in the tool shed?*" Captain Shithead asks.

"*Of course. Why else did you prepare it.*" Commander Ghafour snaps irritably. "*Make sure she has air. I want her alive.*"

"*Yes sir.*" The men do not even try to hide from Nell what they are saying, communicating freely over the common frequency in Arabic. They may not realize her visor can translate or don't care.

The rover stops alongside a non-pressurized metal shed. The captain carries Nell into the shed and drops her to the floor.

"*Is the shed completely empty?*" He gives the interior a quick look, opening and closing cabinets and the storage locker. He had told his men to clean it out but they sometimes slack off and it's his butt if something goes wrong.

"*Yes Captain,*" the soldier said.

"*And the door can be locked?*"

"*Yes Captain, everything is ready. She cannot escape,*" the man reassures his doubting superior.

Nell hasn't moved since the fall and is apparently remains unconscious. The captain uses his toe to roll her over on her back. He leans down twisting her arm to expose the small panel at her wrist. Popping it open, he looks at the vacsuit's readouts, making sure she's alive and has air. He could not care less about any possible broken bones or concussion she may have suffered but he does care that she's breathing when Commander Ghafour calls for her. Almost as an afterthought, he removes the fuel cell that powers her communications, isolating her as completely as any human in history.

Satisfied, he leaves Nell sprawled on the cold stone floor.

ℛℒ

The question of what role the moon plays has been around since the first ancestor looked up with enough intelligence to ask it. At one time or another, the moon has been blamed for crime sprees, bad politicians, crop failures, girl babies and many other equally ridiculous assertions. A medieval book called it the *land of demons* while another claimed it was the *face of God*. Only in the last century has mankind been able to travel there, first sending machines, then going in person. In the late 1960's the Lunar Orbiter series visually mapped the surface down to a meter resolution in preparation for the Apollo lunar landings, which returned almost 400 kilograms of rock samples from six different sites.

In 1994, Clementine orbited Luna hundreds of times while mapping the surface using the next generation of remote sensors. During its two-month voyage, it discovered ice at the lunar South Pole. Four years later Lunar Prospector provided global maps of elemental distribution on the lunar surface using a Gamma Ray Spectrometer and a Neutron Spectrometer. In the early decades of the 21st century, the Badger series of remote controlled lunar prospectors paved the way for the manned expeditions that followed, culminating in the establishment of Shennong in 2016, Kyoto in 2021 and Aldrin Station in 2024.

The Central Highlands is one of the most intensely studied regions on Luna. Consisting of blowout material from four major craters, it's over three-kilometers thick in spots and a rich source of ancient ice, some ore as high as forty percent water. This ice is 4.3 billion years old, trapped in the original cataclysm that ripped the moon from Mother Earth. The meteor impacts that made Alphonsus, Albategnius, Arzachel, and Ptolemaeus craters, brought it within reach of humanity.

Regolith, the powdery layer of material pulverized by the bombardment of micrometeorites over an unimaginable long span of time, averages thirty meters deep over much of the Highlands. In some places, it's composed entirely of anorthite, a mineral consisting of aluminum, calcium, silicon and oxygen, with the chemical formula of $CaAl_2Si_2O_8$. Strip mine operations go after the richest regions using either draglines or bucket loaders to harvest the ore. These huge machines, made entirely from metal smelted in Benjamin Franklin, pull in and store the powdery regolith in enormous bins. When full, convoys pull under them and fill up. A single ore convoy can provide enough tonnage to keep a refinery busy for a week.

Dakota freehold operates Falconhead, the largest anorthite refinery in Benjamin Franklin. Of the many items produced at Falconhead, Calconn superconductors are its specialty, a material in high demand back on Mother Earth but very dangerous to manufacture. Falconhead's location put it close to the supply of raw material coming in from the Central Highlands and far enough away that if it explodes, it would not take Aldrin Station with it.

It requires many layers of organization to keep the Calconn production system functioning. A key element is delivering ore to the refineries in a predictable and timely fashion. Several independent companies collect anorthite from mines all across the Central Highlands and deliver it to Benjamin Franklin. Among these, Surface Master Trucking is by far the largest.

SMT is more than just a trucking company. It maintains facilities in many of the mines, Far Point being the largest, and its contribution to surface roads is substantial. In some cases, SMT vehicles comprise over 95% of a roads usage. Thus, the company is responsible for maintaining a vast system of improved roads encompassing over 90,000 square kilometers. Road crews far outnumber truck drivers.

Imam Abu Bakr looks up at Malik and asks in Arabic. *"You are sure they suspect nothing?"* He sips from a glass of wine imported at great expense from the vineyards of his native Turkey. His own battle helmet sits on the stone table beside him, the half-empty wine decanter next to it.

Malik shrugs, *"They suspect everything and nothing. They are jumpy from the hospital bombing but that is what was intended? Yes? Get them to spread themselves thin?"*

"…and our men are ready?"

"Yes Imam. The men are more than ready. They are tired of driving trucks and road work." Malik growls. His official rank within the army is captain but very few use it in addressing him. He prefers it that way, just as long as they obey his orders.

"And the packages are on schedule? Are you prepared to unload the ship when it arrives?" Imam Bakr strokes his beard.

Malik nods, *"The devices will immediately be brought here and loaded on the trucks. The task force commanders are all true believers and understand when to use the weapons."*

"Allah be praised," Imam Bakr said. *"I pray you are right."*

From his office balcony, the Imam overlooks hundreds of Goliaths and modified ore carriers spread across the vast space. Those in the center have men and machines swarming over them. More Goliaths line each wall, their alterations complete. Normally, there are only a few dozen trucks here at a time, but today is special. SMT drivers from all over the Highlands have converged on Little America bringing in most of the company's 22,000 employees and all of its trucks. Another 18,000 soldiers have arrived from Al Fahad. They're in nearby habitats preparing to board the convoys when the time comes. Soon all will be ready.

Over the last two years, SMT's entire fleet of Goliaths has had power production substantially increased. Under maximum current draw, their high capacity fuel cells can produce over ten megawatts. A typical convoy requires only a fraction of that, leaving the remaining to power laser cannons.

Here and in other facilities under their control, they have modified hundreds of carriers to transport humans, not ore. Each carrier is capable of supporting fifty soldiers and their equipment in the harsh lunar environment. After years of preparation, the Brotherhood is almost ready for battle.

Imam Bakr walks briskly across the expansive floor with Malik at his heels. He wants to check personally that the men are carrying out his orders. The clank of metal against metal competes against the whine of overhead cranes and power tools. Most of the soldiers are lounging outside their troop carriers, their gear already stowed. No one is wearing battle helmets, enjoying one last respite. Nobody knows how long they'll wear them once the fighting begins.

Halfway along their route, they hear the boisterous cries of men and the sharp ring of steel striking steel. It comes from the center of a large gathering of soldiers. Their backs are to Imam Bakr and Malik as they approach.

"*Make way.*" Malik barks in Arabic.

The soldiers, suddenly aware of Imam Bakr, scramble to make a path. In the center of the makeshift arena, two men are circling one another, each swinging the curved steel of a scimitar. The larger of the two fighters glances furtively at Malik and the Imam. That's all the opening his smaller opponent needs. Quick as a cobra, the man's sword leaps out striking the other just above his armored shoulder. The blade bites deep into his neck between the rows of plating. With a gurgling sound and a gush of blood, the man slumps to the floor.

"*Basayev.*" Malik roars, springing forward to kneel beside the fallen soldier. There's nothing to do for him. He's with Allah. The blade had sliced through the jugular and severed his spine. He was dead before he hit the floor.

Standing and facing the young killer, Malik makes sure he's beyond the reach of the scimitar, "*You fool. We are preparing for battle and you kill one of your comrades.*" Malik's voice is hard as the bloody steel in Basayev's hand. His own hand rests lightly on his pistol. Calmness descends upon him.

"*It was an accident.*" the young man growls while blood drips from his sword, pooling at his feet. The chemical rush of making a kill flows through him like an electric current. He's slow to recognize the threat Malik represents.

"*If you weren't the grand nephew of the Caliph, I would kill you myself.*" Malik said, his body tense.

"*I tell you, it was an accident.*" the young man repeats vehemently but without conviction. He will remember this insult. No one talks to him in this way and lives.

"*That is enough,*" Imam Bakr realizes what's about to happen, even if this brash young aristocrat did not. Reporting the death of his nephew to the Caliph is not something one does if they value their life.

With a disgusted snarl Malik said, "*Go back to your unit and prepare to fight. Allah willing, you will be killed during the coming battle.*" Malik keeps his eyes on Basayev and his hand near his pistol. The young man wipes the blood from his scimitar, grins, and stalks away. Turning to the gathered soldiers, he orders. "*Go. All of you. Return to your units. May Allah grant you victory.*"

Malik watches as the men scuffle away, many with fierce hard stares promising revenge against the young Basayev, nephew or not.

Imam Bakr comes forward to stand beside Malik. "As you say, Captain, the men are ready to fight." he said coldly in perfect English.

Two hundred meters away the main airlock opens and another truck enters pulling its carriers. A floor worker guides the vehicle to a clear spot. Seconds after it stops, men and equipment pour out of its interior, while others converge and begin adding armament, preparing another killing machine for the coming harvest.

ЯL

Nell grits her teeth and pulls herself up. She stands still until her head stops spinning. Limping around the interior, she verifies what the bugeye told Captain Shithead. She can't find a single item in the shed, nothing in the cabinets or in the metal locker standing against the back wall. Nell concludes that the windowless building is the perfect prison.

Then she spots a small round hole no bigger than her thumb in the eaves above the door and to the side. She will need to climb up on the workbench to see out of it.

She turns around, places her hands on the counter behind her and does a little jump, planting her butt on the workbench. Leaning back, she uses the empty shelves to pull herself up without putting undue stress on her sore leg. Despite her best efforts, pain shoots through her knee. There might be something wrong there after all.

The hole was punched through the metal from the outside leaving its inner edges sharp and dangerous to her civilian vacsuit. Now is not the time to spring a leak. She presses the bubble of her helmet against the jagged opening. The size of the hole allows only one sensor to peer through it at a time, making it hard for her to discern depth and severely restricting her field of view.

Even with these limitations, Nell can see Evolution's Child and the CUV parked next to it, its crane fully deployed. Already several large crates sit on Luna soil. There are figures in the cargo bay and more on the ground working in and around the now open crates. From this distance and angle, she can't make out what's inside.

Nell's rage soars when she sees a bugeye emerge from her ship's pilothouse, the same airlock she had used just a short time before. The grotesque figure moves around the railed catwalk and climbs up the ladder, joining those working in the cargo bay.

Nell takes a deep breath, calming herself. What are the facts? Her ship contains thirty tons of cargo listed as mining equipment but at this point, Nell seriously doubts that. Who in their right mind would treat her this way after she delivers them a load of mining gear? No, it had to contain something else, but how can that be? She herself had scanned the crates and verified the contents. Her mind chases that fact around before finally concluding that somehow, she'd been fooled.

She turns her thoughts to the men themselves. Despite the armored vacsuits and fancy titles, the lack of discipline makes her doubt these men are military. That leaves only terrorists.

Without the freighter's AI constantly updating her visor, Nell loses track of time. Over the next few hours, she continues to watch and think as Ghafour's crew reshuffles the cargo. Finally, they close the crates and return them to the freighter's cargo bay. Whatever's going on, it's ending.

But as time goes by, Nell convinces herself they must have forgotten her. At last, a rover comes into sight. It pulls up and stops outside the shed. Nell jumps down from the workbench jarring her knee. Knowing she's powerless against even one soldier in a combat suit, she stands calmly in the center of the shed waiting for the door to open.

A bugeye enters the room alert for any surprises. A second bugeye enters more leisurely, coming to a stop in front of Nell. Reaching out, he grasps her wrist and violently twists it around. While Nell grimaces in pain, he deftly installs the fuel cell restoring her communications.

"Pilot, you will do exactly as I tell you or you will die. Is that clear?" Commander Ghafour's voice informs her.

Nell nods inside the clear bubble of her helmet. Her arm feels like it's being wrenched from its socket.

"Excellent."

She isn't sure if this bugeye trying to remove her arm is Ghafour or one of his hoods. Not that it matters. Just before he releases her, Nell notices a small Black Widow symbol with a tiny red hourglass painted on his armored breastplate right at eye level.

Nell's allowed to walk unhindered from the shed. Outside next to the rover are two more bugeyes. It unnerves her to know they can see her but she can't see them. At this close range, their multifaceted sensor arrays eerily cast tiny reflections almost as if they were alive. All of them tower over Nell making her feel small and helpless.

Nell takes the seat furthest from the driver at the back of the rover. The other four bugeyes take seats between her and the door. Past them and over the shoulder of the driver Nell can see a thin slice out the front window, enough to realize they're heading back to Evolution's Child.

Nell cycles through the airlock staring at that tiny spider with its little red hourglass. Sharing the tight confines of the little airlock with this armored bugeye almost brings Nell to the breaking point. She welcomes the return of sound as air pressure floods back. The familiar squeal of the airlock door comforts her.

Stepping into her inner sanctum, she's shocked to see her control room in such disarray. The main computer cabinet is wide open and a skinny bearded young man wearing old-fashioned wire-framed glasses is sitting cross-legged on the floor in front of it. Strewn around him is an assortment of electronic gear and testing equipment. He's also the first person Nell's observed not wearing a combat vacsuit. He looks up and grins.

Nell removes her helmet, "What are you doing to my ship?" She asked, surveying the mess. A second AI is on the floor next to the man, its carbon fiber case unmistakable.

"We are upgrading your AI," a familiar voice said from behind her. "I could not trust our cargo to your primitive program."

Nell wheels around. Ghafour is standing in the doorway leading to her living quarters. The man is in his late forties, tall with black hair and dark eyes. A short beard gives him a rough appearance. A hairless line draws attention to a scar across his right cheek. Arrogance permeates the air around him.

"It got your cargo this far," Nell retorts.

Ghafour's eyes narrow down to slits and his mouth forms into a humorless hard line. His tone leaves no doubt as to who's in charge.

"Quiet. Follow me." Ghafour orders and turns away, heading deeper into Nell's home.

When Nell hesitates, she receives a violent push from behind. She sails through the doorway and sprawls onto the padded floor at the feet of Ghafour.

"*Remove her visor and suit.*" Ghafour orders gruffly.

Spiderman promptly reaches down, grasps the hard point behind Nell's neck, and lifts her. His armored hands are rough but efficient in removing her backpack but when he reaches for her visor, Nell removes it herself, handing the device to Ghafour. As Spiderman continues to pull at her suit she said, "Slow down. I'll take it off."

She might as well be talking to the wall. Spiderman continues until Nell is standing in only panties and tank top. Nell notices Ghafour's sudden interest in her, like a hungry carnivore coming across a fresh piece of meat.

In her youth, Nell worked as an exotic dancer in the clubs along Stanwell Moor Road just outside Heathrow International Spaceport. Back then it was an area that catered to business travelers. She had made excellent money flashing her green eyes up at the johns. At only 165 centimeters, all of them towered over her, bringing out either the protector or the dominator in every man. It didn't hurt that she had firm tits, slender waist, and a great ass. That was another life, before she met James and fell in love, before the girls and that terrible afternoon.

The medical treatments she periodically receives in Aldrin Station not only maintains the calcium in her bones, it gives her great muscle tone, and Luna's light gravity helps even more. Nell recognizes the look and realizes this may be her best chance regardless of how revolting. Sexual intrigue was something she'd been good at long ago but the thought sickens her now. Recognizing the opening is one thing, being willing to exploit it quite another.

Ghafour licks his lips and openly leers at her breasts. She's not wearing a bra and they stretch the thin fabric of her top clearly displaying her erect nipples. Nell knows from experience what's going though his head, the rationalization males go through when the chemicals in their brains start clamoring for sex. It's hard to resist hundreds of millions of years of evolution. She flips her hair back and runs her hand through its mass, letting it cascade over bare shoulders and hard nipples.

"Search everything. Remove anything that can be used as a weapon," Ghafour orders hoarsely. Spiderman immediately moves to comply. Nell can only watch helplessly as the bugeye begins ransacking her home.

The young man in the control room has stopped and is eyeballing Nell's curves in obvious appreciation. From his seat, Ghafour calls roughly in an unknown language, *"Get back to work."*

Nell believes he's speaking Arabic but without her visor, she's not sure. Gathering her courage, She asked in her best damsel-in-distress voice, "Commander, please tell me what you're doing?"

"Kneel, here in front of me. No man should have to look up to a woman." Dropping to her knees, Nell shows plenty of cleavage and spreads her legs slightly as she settles back on her butt.

Just looking at her sends the juices flowing through Ghafour and he begins thinking with his little head, "I need to use your little ship for a few days, that's all," he said letting his eyes roam over her body, "You will be back in command before you know it."

"Can you at least tell me where we're going?" She asks with as much innocence as she can muster, resisting the urge to puke. It would spoil her performance.

Ghafour hesitates for a moment, considering the many things he would like to do to this beautiful infidel. "We will make a brief stop at Aldrin Station then on to Luna orbit where we will dock with a waiting spaceliner. Then you can go about your business." He's pleased with himself.

Nell manages to hold down her last meal. Even without her visor, she knows Ghafour is lying but he's one smooth bastard.

"What have I brought you?" She asked, not really expecting an answer.

Ghafour hesitates. He normally would not answer any questions but there's something about this woman. "Specialized mining equipment for a job in the asteroid belt." His expression hardens as his mind veers away from sex. "Enough questions. you will contact Luna Central at Aldrin Station and tell them this freighter will be landing for fuel before proceeding on to orbit," he leaves no room for argument.

Nell flirts with the idea of refusing but that would be taking the easy way out. "LC will need a new flight plan and the amount of fuel," Nell said, a plan beginning to take shape.

Ghafour's cold smile is a brilliant white line cutting through his beard. He's killed many times and thrives on the power it gives him. He must now rein in that animal instinct and use the wits Allah gave him to mold this woman to his needs.

"You will oversee the calculations and as for fuel, I only care that we have enough to get to lunar orbit. After that, you're on your own." Ghafour leans forward intently, bringing his face within centimeters of Nell's. His breath smells of wine and garlic. "One mistake, one slip of the tongue, one stray gesture, and I will cut your head off very slowly."

She shudders involuntarily, drops her eyes, and meekly nods. At that moment, Nell is convinced this man has done it before and will not hesitate to do it again.

Ghafour revels in his power over her. Western women are so easy. They crave the discipline he brings. Again, sexual fantasies spring unbidden into his mind. His blood runs hot.

"I will need my AI to fly the ship," Nell said as docilely as she can manage.

"You will use ours," Ghafour said ogling her cleavage, watching them rise and fall with each breath.

"A new AI must be fully tested. That takes weeks," Nell insists.

Ghafour's voice grows hard, "You will use ours. I have been given assurances it can fly this freighter."

Nell remains quiet, but ever so subtly, she shakes her head, the look on her face clearly said *'you have been lied to.'*

"*Ahmed. Come here.*" Ghafour calls out in Arabic.

The young man looks up in fear. What has he done now? He scrambles off the floor and hurries into the room his eyebrows knotted in a worried frown. His unkempt black hair sticks out in all directions.

"Commander?" He asked.

"*Is your AI installed?*" Ghafour demands.

The man glances at Nell, "Yes, Commander. I'm running final tests right now," he replies, realizing he made a mistake in speaking English. Ahmed was born in London and spoke nothing but English until he was almost twenty. As a result, the others do not consider him an equal.

"Have you found the anomaly in the fuel injectors?" Nell asks. "This ship has new thrusters and it took the shipyard a week to get them calibrated. How can you install a new AI without starting even one thruster?" Her voice rises slightly, "This is an old freighter. You can't just come in here and toss in a new AI. It won't work."

Ghafour reaches out and grabs a handful of Nell's raven black hair, forcing her to arch her back. Staring intently into her green eyes, He asked softly, "Why not pilot?"

His stale breath is hot on Nell's cheek. She begins breathing in short quick gulps, her pupils dilating as she struggles to hold fear in check. "Over time an AI learns to compensate for the wear of a pump and the peculiarities of a thruster. A new AI won't know any of it. The ship will tear itself apart before we get off the ground."

This is it, the big lie. She desperately needs her own AI. It's her best, perhaps only, chance to do something.

Ghafour releases Nell and leans back. Looking up at Ahmed he raises his eyebrows skeptically and asks, "*What do you say Ahmed? Will your AI damage this ship?*"

Ahmed frowns, looking fearfully at Ghafour, "*Commander, I am a programmer. This is more of an engineering question. Perhaps we should ask Khalid?*" he said in broken Arabic.

Ghafour cultivates fear in others. He can't help himself. It's his way of maintaining command. "*Khalid is busy. I am asking you, Ahmed,*" he said coldly in perfect Arabic. He's just about had enough of this sniveling technocrat with his western education.

"*Yes Commander.*" Ahmed stammers. "Ah… *all the ships systems are controlled by the AI… and it is capable of adapting … theoretically it is possible.*" He can't look Ghafour in the eye.

Without her visor, Nell can't understand what they're saying but it's obvious that Ghafour isn't happy with his man. Nell dares to hope and decides to go for broke. "My AI is the original install in the ship over fifteen years ago. You cannot replace her without extensive testing and recalibration." She keeps her eyes on the floor. "You'll kill us all."

Ahmed remains quiet, not daring to meet the glare of his commander. He cursed his fortune for the thousandth time. He doesn't know the details of the mission and doesn't want to know. It's his job to set up the AI on the ship, not troubleshoot the mechanicals. He's never been good with his hands. That was the main reason he had gone into programming in the first place.

"*Hook both up together,*" Ghafour orders irritably, to him an obvious and simplistic solution.

"*Ah… sir, that is not… ah… recommended,*" Ahmed stammers.

"*Why.*" Ghafour demands.

"*There can be only one AI in control, just as there is only one Commander. If there were two, which would we obey? One of them must have ultimate command, eliminating the need for the other. Anything else would cause complete confusion the first time they didn't agree. The system would lock up.*" Ahmed said in a rush, relieved the conversation is back to something familiar.

Ghafour curses the incompetence around him. As usual, he must improvise deep in a mission. He looks down at the female, confident in his mastery over her. "*Remove your AI. Replace it with the original.*" Ghafour growls at Ahmed. "*Now go. Get out of my sight.*"

Ahmed backs through the control room door, his face a mixture of relief and concern. "*As you wish.*" It's not his place to question the Commander even though he's sure his AI could adapt to this freighter, but he's too weak to make the case. It's easier to do as Ghafour orders, safer too.

"You shall have your AI, but what will I get in return?" Ghafour asks the woman kneeling before him.

Nell remains silent, head bowed, not daring to look up.

Spiderman finishes ransacking Nell's home and returns. The bugeye is carrying a disrupter sidearm and two power packs. He shows them to Commander Ghafour.

"*Secure them. Then go help Khalid with the package. Let me know if there are any problems, otherwise, don't bother me,*" Ghafour orders.

The bugeye leaves. Ghafour rises and steps around Nell, closing the control room door. Coming back, he stops behind her. She doesn't move but is intensely aware of where he is.

Reaching down Ghafour grasps Nell's hair once again, pulling her up. He bends her head back exposing her neck. Thrusting his face over her shoulder, he licks Nell's cheek right below her ear. She utters a frightened gasp and groans as he begins to grope her. Ghafour laughs coldly and Nell knows it's time to pay the piper…

ЯL

Ahmed looks up when the door opens. The odor of sex instantly permeates the control room. He can hardly take his eyes off her breasts. A trickle of blood runs from Nell's nostril. She swipes at it with the back of her hand, smearing red across her cheek. She looks crushed, her spirit broken, ashamed to meet Ahmed's gaze.

"*Is the AI ready?*" Ghafour asks almost pleasantly from behind her. He's wallowing in the aftermath of ejaculation. It's a gift from Allah that she's here, available to him, giving him a jump on paradise. Too bad she wasn't a virgin, but what western woman is.

"*Yes commander. We haven't run any tests but that shouldn't be necessary,*" Ahmed said.

51

"Watch the pilot carefully. She is going to set up the flight calculations. Make sure that is all she does." Ghafour orders.

"As you wish." Ahmed leers as Nell takes the pilot's seat. The man cannot tear his eyes off her bare tits and hard nipples.

Nell felt marginally better in the familiar surroundings of the control room, sitting in the command chair, the bank of controls and readouts spread out before her. She reaches out and activates the control room speaker. "Emcee, are you there?" She asked, casually letting her hands grip the padded armrest of the chair. There are no apparent controls in the armrest and the movement looks completely innocent.

"Aye Nell, I'm here. What happened?" the AI is confused. It's unaccustomed to having memory gaps.

"I will explain later. Right now, we need to change our flight plan. Access standard flight equations Z115." Being a lone woman plying the trade routes between Mother Earth and Luna, Nell has set up an elaborate emergency system. Between the pressure sensors installed in the armrest and verbal keywords, Nell can communicate just about any command to Emcee without anyone being the wiser. It's one of the games she and the AI play during the long hours between stops, each trying to come up with a scenario that isn't covered. This is the first major test and there isn't any room for error.

"Roger Nell, Z115 loaded," Emcee said.

So far so good. Without looking up She asked, "Commander, is there a particular orbit we need to reach?"

"Take on fuel at Little America for a two hundred kilometer circular orbit in Earth-Luna plane," Ghafour said.

With Ahmed hovering over her shoulder, Nell plunges on. "Emcee, our new destination is Little America, any available dock. Use a standard parabolic trajectory at sixty percent efficiency and economy at seventy-five. We will take on fuel for a round trip to Taurus, any two-zero-zero planer orbit. Ask for the soonest available launch window. Clear?"

"Aye," Emcee said.

"Commence" Nell allows herself a glance at Ghafour, receiving a cold stare in return. She takes grim satisfaction thinking about what she had just arranged for him, but she mustn't give it away. She lets her eyes drop.

"How long will this take?" Ghafour asks, recovered to the point of fantasizing again, building up for another go at her.

"About five minutes," Nell answers.

"Go get cleaned up. You will need to transfer the information to Luna Central," Ghafour orders.

Nell rises and goes back through her quarters heading for the washroom. She leaves the door open giving Ghafour and Ahmed a fine view of the proceedings. Hesitating at the mirror, Nell sees the smear of blood on her cheek. Her head starts spinning and her stomach churns. She just manages to get a utility bag before barfing into it. Wiping her mouth with a towel, she hears laughter.

Sending the bag down the waste chute, she strips off her panties and enters the shower. Warm air and water droplets flow over her head cascading down her body. The little electric motor that runs the fan is ancient and makes a high pitch whine.

As she soaps up, she risks a covert glance through the clear shower wall. Even though the clear plastic distorts them, she can clearly see both men staring at her. Turning her back to them, she leans over giving them a good look at her ass while scrubbing hard between her legs.

"Emcee, can you hear me?" Nell barely whispers, almost matching the pitch of the shower fan.

"Aye, I hear you. Please verify general order 115," the AI asks almost too faint for Nell to hear over the fan.

"General order 115 verified. Authority code Nell, Z7592."

A moment later Ghafour throws open the stall door. "You are finished." He roughly pulls her out of the shower.

Nell grabs some coveralls as Ghafour pushes her out of the bathroom and into her quarters. She makes sure her tits bounce, and meekly asks, "May I put my clothes on?"

Ghafour hands Nell a towel, his nostrils flaring as he catches a whiff of wet hair. "Yes… you must look presentable when you talk with Luna Central. Go ahead, dress."

She gives a good show as she slips first one leg, then the other, into the coveralls. Extending both arms behind her, she arches her back and slides them in, pulling the material over her shoulders. Already hard from the cool air, her nipples rub against the thin fabric and swell even larger. She fastens the buttons up the front, leaving the last three open.

Nell remains submissive, never letting her eyes meet theirs, afraid she would give herself away.

The cycling of the airlock signals someone entering. Two bugeyes emerge and Nell wonders how they both had fit in the small chamber. They pass through the control room and enter the living area. Nell moves to stand behind Ghafour, not finding it particularly difficult to act frightened of these figures.

"*Are you finished?*" Ghafour asks, pleased that Nell looks to him for protection, another sign of his dominance over her.

Both bugeyes nod then begin to remove their helmets. Nell is surprised when Spiderman turns out to be a woman. She's hard with a perpetual scowl beneath raven black hair cut short. The other bugeye is an older man, his hair and beard salted with gray, his eyes tired and movements slow.

"*All is ready Commander,*" the old man said in Arabic.

"*Allah be praised,*" turning to Nell, "You will make that call now, pilot." He steps aside motioning her to enter the control room.

Ghafour waits at the doorway and Ahmed moves out of the camera's field of view as Nell takes the command seat. This will be the last time she will sit here.

"Emcee, hail Luna Central," she orders.

"Aye, hailing," is the cheery response.

A moment later, "This is Luna Central. How may I aid you?" The uniformed officer on the main screen looks mighty good to Nell. If only you were here, you and some of your friends.

"This is Evolution's Child submitting a change in flight plans. Downloading the new flight calculations now... I'm standing by." She sits back, even remembering to place her hands just as she had done before.

"Roger, Evolution's Child standing by..."

Nell keeps her eyes on the officer as he inputs her calculations, not risking even a glance at the other occupants in the room. True to form, they were correct.

"Your request for fuel has been approved. I have you arriving at Little America, Dock 14 in approximately thirty-two minutes. Evolution's Child, you are good for launch in T minus four minutes." In all her years of piloting, she never felt as completely alone as she did when that figure disappears.

Nell sits still for a moment wondering if she's doing the right thing. Her mind can reach only one conclusion. She's certain at this point that these men are religious extremists bent on some violent mission, what exactly, she does not know, but big, really big.

Everyone has seen the face of terrorism, the planes flying into the Twin Towers, the mushroom cloud over Houston, and countless body bags lining the cities sidewalks. These visions of death are part of modern life, but it's the specter of her dead daughter's that fuel Nell's nightmares and steadies her resolve now.

"Come. You are no longer needed here," Ghafour declares. He's pleased at her performance and plans to show her how much during the flight. In his arrogance, he actually believes Nell will welcome his attentions.

Ghafour follows Nell into her quarters, grasps the front of her coveralls and pulls her to him. "You did well." He leers as more and more of her tits emerge from confinement.

Nell battles to maintain the charade. The smoking school bus burns in her mind, even as she reaches out to stroke his manhood.

ЯL

The wail of the acceleration klaxon jolts Nell. Has it only been three minutes? It seems much longer. Nell lay unabashedly naked, sprawled on her back, staring up at the padded ceiling. Ghafour lies beside her heaving and gasping for breath. The deed had been fast and furious, Nell had made sure of that.

Khalid kneels on the floor next to the open control room door. As Ghafour raped Nell for the second time, Khalid had cast a few furtive glances and then continued his incantation, rocking back and forth, touching his forehead to the floor. Nell thinks it's a prayer and almost pities him. He's a frightened old man.

Although she had kept her eyes shut throughout most of the assault, Nell had caught Ahmed watching from the control room. He looks like he has something to say but is afraid to say it.

Ghafour sighs deeply and opens his eyes, his face glistening with sweat. Looking up at Ahmed, he said, "*Sit down. We are about to launch.*"

Ahmed enters the living room and makes for the only other padded chair aboard the ship, still staring at Nell, "*Not there, you idiot. Go and sit next to Khalid.*"

Nell can see Spiderwoman sitting in her command chair and feels a rush of resentment. Spiderwoman glances up and catches Nell watching her. She grins cruelly but something in Nell's expression wipes it off her face. She glances nervously down at the controls and back up at the pilot. Now it's Nell's turn to smile.

56

"Ten," Emcee announces.

Of the four aboard Evolution's Child, only Ghafour had been offworld before this mission. The others rely on him for guidance.

"Nine."

"*Commander.*" It's the first time Nell has heard the female's voice. It's harsh and full of malice.

"Eight."

Ghafour sits up hearing panic in Spiderwoman's voice. She is staring at Nell.

"Seven."

Turning, Ghafour looks down at Nell lying on the bed. She coldly meets his gaze. The total absence of fear shocks him. In its place is only disgust.

"Six."

"*Stop the countdown.*" Ghafour yells to Spiderwoman.

"Computer, stop." The woman commands in bad English. Leaning forward, she frantically begins flipping switches and twisting knobs, not knowing what any of them did.

"Five."

Nell grins contemptuously, never breaking eye contact with Ghafour.

"Four."

"*Stop. Stop.*" Spiderwoman demands even louder.

Nell chuckles in triumph.

"What have you done." Ghafour demands.

"Three."

In the control room, Spiderwoman goes berserk, striking the command panel using all the armored might of her combat vacsuit. The impact folds the panel in the middle, ripping it away from the wall. Glass, plastic and bits of metal fly around the control room like a hive of Africanized bees.

Rising, Ghafour jerks at his trousers trying to pull them up as he heads for the control room.

"Two."

Spiderwoman raises her arms for another blow when it occurs to her that the AI's CPU might be the better target.

"*Help her.*" Ghafour yells at Ahmed who simply lays his head back against the wall, a resigned look in his eyes as he gazes at the naked figure of Nell, strangely pleased that this wisp of a woman has gotten the best of Commander Ghafour. He figures if something is amiss, there's nothing he can do about it now. Might as well enjoy the view on his way to paradise.

"One."

Spiderwoman is on this mission because she's one of the fastest draws in the kingdom, a fact that caused more than a little consternation among the men. She has many kills and is confident that she will be victorious on this day as well. Drawing her sidearm as she turns, her brain is sending the impulse to her trigger finger when acceleration squeezes them in its iron grip.

Rising up through the metal ship, the sound of the new Pratt and Whitney's going to full throttle destroys the unprotected hearing of the four terrorists and Nell. The acceleration compresses Ahmed's spine and his neck vertebra splinters impaling his scull on his spinal cord. His internal organs rip away and compact at the bottom of his body cavity, the heart crushing everything beneath it.

The acceleration catches Khalid on the forward swing of his chant, leaning down but before his forehead touched the floor. From just a few centimeters away, his face slams into the padding with the force of a cannon shot and his spine shatters in a dozen places, snapping like a brittle twig. Pain sears through his body in one blazing jolt as his heart and lungs flatten against his ribs.

Spiderwoman never realizes she lost. Her upper body collapses down on shattered legs and both arms slam to the floor, the disrupter still clenched in her hand. Her head falls furthest and attains the highest velocity. Impact with the floor shatters her skull like a rotten egg. There's no bouncing, everything simply hits and sticks to the floor as though coated with Velcro.

The acceleration drives Ghafour into the floor like a carpenter driving a nail. His hip and knee joints separate as he collapses. His torso stays upright when his butt hits the floor, one thigh in front and the other behind. His lower legs twist grotesquely underneath his body and his internal organs compress into a mass. His backbone shatters and his shoulders spiral downward coming to rest unnaturally close to his hips.

Just before liftoff, Nell tenses her body in anticipation. She thought she would have about three seconds at this G load before the blood completely drained from her brain and she loses consciousness. That proved to be grossly optimistic. Under the tremendous acceleration, Nell's heart burst, her brain pancakes, and her lower jaw wrenches open slamming into her collapsing breastbone. She's dead in an instant.

Designed for propulsion components available twenty years before, Evolution's Child was never meant to handle accelerations of this magnitude. The ship's light cargo and almost empty fuel tanks exacerbate the situation, further elevating the G load. Even the most junior engineer in the Hyundai shipyards could have predicted what came next.

The welds along the titanium struts that transfer the loads from the port thruster to the ship's superstructure fail along one side magnifying the strain on the remaining supports. The fuel feed lines twist and rupture mixing the hypergolic liquids which ignite spontaneously. Systems designed to shut down fail and fuel continues to feed the fire.

Emcee tries to compensate for the loss of the thruster. Systems never designed for this level of acceleration begin to fail. Evolution's Child rolls progressing rapidly to an out-of-control spiral.

Hypergolic fuels spewing from the ruptured lines mix and create a fiery plume in the ships wake. Evolution's Child never gets higher than a few thousand meters, her trajectory a blazing arc north northwest of Alphonsus crater.

A trucker plying the Trans Lunar Highway a few hours out of Summerhaven is amazed to see the burning meteor silently streak across the sky, disappearing over the horizon and into the Sea of Clouds.

Eye of the Hurricane

"Man is a Religious Animal. He is the only Religious Animal.
He is the only animal that has the True Religion -- several of
them. He is the only animal that loves his neighbor as himself
and cuts his throat if his theology isn't straight."

Mark Twain (1835-1910)

Security Chief Corso Dugan scans the room as the heavy airlock door slides shut behind him. He thinks of the Regional Command Center as a calm center walled in by the raging storm. His troops call it the Bull's Eye.

The RCC is a circular amphitheater. At its focal point is a large dais. Surrounding the dais in five concentric rings are workstations, each composed of a large rectangular slab of Duraglass laid flat like a tabletop. Within these slabs is a three dimensional network of micro-imagers designed to process huge amounts of data.

Data mining is something every Lunarian knows to one extent or another, the straightforward evolution of the search engine of last century applied to the tremendous amount of real-time information collected today. Operators stand at their posts, hands darting over their workstations, sifting through this vast quantity of information, only managing to observe a very small percentage of the total.

Magi carries the bulk of the workload. She juxtaposes real-time data with the ever-expanding database of human knowledge using sophisticated algorithms. She compares what is, with what was. Just as a hunter waits patiently for movement in the distant stand of trees to signal the arrival of quarry, so too does the AI look for anomalies in the data using comparative analysis.

After a quick head count, Corso is satisfied his RCC is fully manned. Other operators link in from all over Luna, but the citizens in this room are his handpicked crew.

"Chief on deck." Captain Ben Dugan calls out.

Just as he's done a thousand times, Corso links his visor to Magi's external data stream. The RCC disappears and he's hovering sixty thousand kilometers above Aldrin Station in open space. Lagrange One Space Station is close by. Corso glances at the station and moves on.

In the western sky is Taurus Colony, 400,000 kilometers ahead of the moon and in the same orbit. Taurus consists of two wheels rotating in opposite directions, each over two kilometers in diameter and connected by a massive cylindrical hub. With an economy based around building and maintaining power satellites, ships swarm around the colony. Corso doesn't spend time here either.

Hyundai Shipyards is 400,000 kilometers behind the moon also in the same orbit. From a distance, it appears a spindly structure haphazardly assembled. Hyundai is a zero G facility with an economy based on shipbuilding. It's the birthplace of every battlestation, frigate, and freighter in the system.

Corso lingers on Hyundai for a moment. The main yard is empty. They completed Battlestation Houris several weeks ago and hadn't started on a new project yet. He had watched for months as they laid the keel and assembled the giant warship. It's one of the largest ever built and used a tremendous amount of Lunarian iron. The Brotherhood hadn't wanted to spend the extra money on titanium. The decision had been a great boon to Aldrin Station's iron industry. Corso just wished he knew where that battlestation was right now.

He sweeps his gaze across the plethora of objects in geosynchronous orbit, orbital power stations beaming energy down to Mother Earth, communications satellites relaying billions of data streams, weather observation platforms and industrial manufacturing facilities, crowd the orbit. In some places, the satellites appear so thick that Corso can imagine stepping from one to the next.

Dropping his gaze lower, he notes several Stratoliners rising up through the atmosphere with another just departing Heaven's Gate on its way back down. Framed against the blue and white Earth, one of the mass drivers in LEO flashes along its length as it injects another Product Delivery Module down through the atmosphere. He stares intently at the PDM and a moment later, a list of what's aboard appears within his visual. It's another delivery of Calconn.

With a flip of his hand, a virtual control panel appears around Corso's waist in a great arc. He activates partial visual, his fingers feeling the pressure of the keystroke, his ears hearing the click. Ben and Major Mallory appear beside him.

"Show me what you've got," Corso orders.

"Fourteen minutes ago we picked up a freighter coming out of Cullman Outpost," Ben said. He zooms across the lunar surface to hover above the small mining community inside Herschel crater. The three watch Evolution's Child launch, pitch over and accelerate, spewing a contrail as it lost control. Its flight path was far enough away that the defensive batteries along the top of Rim Mountain simply locked on and tracked it without firing. Ben maintains perspective on the craft as it penetrates the Sea of Clouds and disappears.

"We don't know exactly where the ship hit, but using the data from the cannon batteries we can calculate it very accurately, assuming constant flight parameters from the last known good measurements," Major Mallory explains. She's a second generation Lunarian, a member of the Turner family. Her calm professional demeanor when under fire has gained her rank and responsibility at a young age.

"The Fitzgerald will be overhead in two minutes and we can do a full visual sweep of the area," Ben said. Named after a ship that plied the Great Lakes over a century before, the Edmund Fitzgerald is a freighter in the Earth/Luna system. Currently, it's ready to break orbit heading for Hyundai Shipyards, its tanks filled with water, its cargo holds with metals and food. It would have broken orbit minutes before but Luna Central held it up on Ben's request.

Reviewing the doomed ship's flight data, Corso said, "Look at the gee loading. Nothing organic could have survived."

Mallory and Ben nod agreement and watch as Corso takes control of the vid, resetting the time back to just before launch and enlarging Cullman outpost. He pulls data from Luna Central and reviews the flight path change requested by the freighter's pilot. Corso senses something is wrong with the woman but can't put his finger on the reason. Probably just the fact her ship had not followed the flight path she herself had submitted. Hindsight is always twenty-twenty.

Corso expands the search for data inside the outpost itself, probing in real-time for an opening into the local network. The firewall he hits is unlike any he's encountered. None of his usual methods so much as dent it. Cullman outpost apparently has something to hide and the resources to do it.

"Assign someone to crack that firewall. I want to see what's going on in Cullman. How soon before we can get a bird overhead? I want an orbital sweep as soon as possible," Corso orders.

"We can divert the Fitzgerald but that would take it out of range of the freighter's impact point," Mallory said.

"No. We need that data. What are our other options?" Corso asks.

"There's a shuttle coming out of Shennong in just over ten minutes. We could divert it enough to side-scan the outpost as it ascends to orbit," Ben suggests.

"Do it," Corso commands. Ben relays the orders to his staff. Turning to Mallory, Corso continues. "I also want all available information on that freighter and what it was carrying, including her pilot." Corso's familiar deep voice inspires confidence in his people and the growing number of citizens linked from afar. This is quickly becoming the top link across the Republic.

"That task is already underway," Mallory said, pauses a moment and said, "The Fitzgerald is coming into position."

The Fitzgerald provides a bird's eye view, as though they are flying above the ill-fated ships trajectory, marked by a thin yellow line below. The three officers wait expectantly for the first signs of the crash.

The tension builds as they approach the projected impact location. The first thing they see is a long gouge down one side of a broad valley. The debris field starts about two-thirds down the slope and continues across the floor. It ends at the remains of the titanium superstructure. It's twisted and bent but somehow, it protected the freighter's pilothouse, more or less. The engines are gone, shredded into thousands of pieces, only the dense hard nozzles remain recognizable. Several cargo crates had skipped across the surface like flat stones across water, their impact points visible for hundreds of meters.

The three officers began independent searches, taking full advantage of the depth of the data flowing in. Each of them approaches the situation from a different angle. Corso finds traces of human remains as he probes what is left of the pilothouse, Ben sweeps for any electronic signal and Mallory looks at the freighter's cargo.

"The site is electronically dead," Ben reports.

"I've got a shipping crate with an anomalous signature," Mallory said. The other two officers link with her. From around the edges of its damaged lid, one of the containers is emitting the barest whisper of energy. Yet, when she scans inside the crate, all that shows is a large industrial check valve, common throughout Luna. It's a mechanical part with no need of an internal power source and thus, there's no reason for energy to be leaking from this shipping crate, but it's hard to argue with facts.

"Can you tell what's generating the signal Magi?" Corso asks.

Magi runs the data through hundreds of different optimizations, comparing it to everything in her database. "Negative, the best I can do is narrow the signature down to a common fuel cell, nothing special about it at all," the AI said.

Still, energy coming from a place where it should not is cause for concern, especially in light of everything that's occurred in the last few days. This entire thing feels wrong to Corso, and he learned long ago to pay attention to his gut.

"We need some eyes out at that crash site ASAP." Corso rumbles to no one in particular.

ЯL

Malik moves swiftly through the office and onto the balcony. Imam Bakr sits watching the preparations taking place on the floor below, a glass of wine in his hand.

"*Yes. What is it?*" the Imam said in Arabic.

"*Imam. The freighter bringing us the bombs has crashed.*" Malik said. He dreads being the one to tell him but learned long ago that it's better to give bad news quickly. Being a cautious man, Malik wears his helmet just in case the Imam flies into one of his fits of rage.

Imam Bakr reaches for his helmet. "*Where did it crash?*" he fumbles at the mechanical seals before finally getting it secure. According to regulations, he should have Malik check it but that seldom happens.

"*Three hundred kilometers out on Mare Nubium,*" Malik said. "*Sensors from the Houris tracked the ship but could not determine why it crashed.*" He feeds the vid to the Imam's helmet. It shows the frantic last flight of Evolution's Child, pinpointing the exact location of her final resting place.

The Imam immediately concludes that someone needs to go out and either retrieve the nukes or destroy them along with any evidence. He doesn't care what happened to the freighter to make it crash and it never occurs to him to consider any survivors that might need help. His mind has moved on, weighing his options, planning what his response should be to minimize this disaster.

Turning back to Malik He asked, *"Do the infidels know of the crash?"*

"I know not of a certainty but it would surprise me if they missed it. They have a very good sensor and communications network and the ship passed just north of Alphonsus crater. It crashed not far from Al Fahad." Malik said.

Al Fahad is the Brotherhood's only city on Luna. Located in the rim of Lassell crater, it lies 240 kilometers southwest of Alphonsus, well out on the Sea of Clouds.

Sheik Mohammad Abas rules Al Fahad with an iron hand. He's undeniably the most powerful Muslim on Luna and he's in a vile mood when Imam Bakr opens a channel to him. He reviews the vid before raising one eyebrow and looking down his long nose at the Imam. *"What is it you would have me to do? I cannot spare any ships."*

The Sheik is dressed traditionally in a gray Imam's overgarment, the white dishadasha visible down the front, and a white shora with a black egal on his head, all of the highest quality. The man's intensity makes Imam Bakr uneasy, reminding him of the depth of his dislike. It's obvious to Imam Bakr that the Sheik will not be doing any fighting today. His men would face death without him.

"Then send trucks and rovers. The crash site is only 135 kilometers from Al Fahad. They can be there in two hours. We cannot allow this shipment to fall into enemy hands." Imam Bakr argues vehemently.

"I agree," Major General Arif joins the conversation. It's his right as Supreme Commander to monitor any communications. He doesn't bother vidcasting, letting his tone convey his displeasure. *"Sheik Abas,*

how many men can you spare?" He asked.

The Sheik sighs in resignation, *"Perhaps twenty."*

"We must secure that cargo. Send a full company of your men and I will supplement them with a frigate from my fleet. If I can spare a ship then you can spare a single company." Unspoken words hang heavy between the men. They all know the Minister insisted on delivering the weapons this way, and none of them, not even Major General Abdel Salam Arif, Supreme Commander of the Islamic Expeditionary Force, has the balls to place the blame at his feet. Too many have died after saying far less.

"As you will," the Sheik bows his head in submission. Only his eyes tell a different tale. Some day he will deal with the arrogant dog, Bakr, permanently.

The General thanks Allah that he had the foresight to transport the warheads in three shipments. The Shennong and Kyoto forces already have theirs. He mentally runs through their location.

"Imam Bakr, we must arm you properly if the will of Allah is to be accomplished... I will have two warheads sent immediately. You should receive them within the hour. Imam, your task remains the same, secure Alphonsus Complex." As Supreme Commander, Major General Arif resents the fact he must nursemaid his subordinates. They know as well as he the importance of maintaining discipline within the plan. *"Allah Akbar,"* he said dismissing them.

"Allah Akbar," they echo, both assuming the General is still listening. Only now, it's no longer Imam Bakr's problem.

"When you have secured the bombs, send them to me. I will proceed as planned," Imam Bakr said.

"Inshallah... As Allah wills," Sheik Abas said before his image disappears, his look that of a lion contemplating a jackal.

ЯL

The department's cafeteria is not a five star restaurant by anyone's definition but the food is hot and plentiful. Brice, Corazon, Tempel, Lazarus, and Kitajima sit at a table against the far wall. The rest of Quan Kiai and about a hundred other police officers are spread out across the room eating and talking quietly. The subdued hum of conversation and the occasional clank from the kitchen provides familiar background to their meal.

Captain Kitajima Osaka makes it a point to eat with his team as often as he can. It gives him a chance to evaluate them outside the training environment and keeps him in touch with their emotional state. He's not interested in their personal problems but is concerned with how well they handle them, and he likes the camaraderie. It reminds him of his days playing professional football.

When Ben vidcasts next to the dining table, he quickly becomes the focal point of everyone present. "Greetings Kitajima. We have a situation out on the Sea of Clouds. View the vid."

Magi is aware of Kitajima's human limitations and adjusts the playback accordingly, increasing the speed in some sections and slowing it down in others, thus allowing him to gather the pertinent facts as fast as his mental processes can manage. She ends it on a close-up of the damaged crate. Lazarus shares the playback with Kitajima but has a hard time keeping up. The images move by too fast for his untrained mind to grasp. For the rest of the platoon, Magi presents it at sixty-times normal speed.

"Corso wants you and your Highlanders to find out what's going on. Captain Marquest will go with you for technical support but you will be in charge. Clear?" Ben said to Kitajima.

"Clear, but Ben, I can handle this without Lindsey. She can link with us when we get there," Kitajima said.

"Corso wants her with you. You may need her engineering skills before this is finished," Ben replies.

"I should go too," Lazarus blurts out, breaking etiquette.

Kitajima turns and looks at him. "What? Why should you go?"

"I know Brotherhood hardware. If the IB is involved in this, I'll be able to help," Lazarus claims.

"He's right," Lindsey said, her image appearing next to Bens. "Taking him along is a good idea."

"He's not yet a full citizen. What if he falls apart on us out there?" Kitajima asks, glancing at the man across the table from him. "No offense," he said.

Lazarus shrugs.

"I'll vouch for him. He performed as well as anyone at the hospital, and he's cleared for surface duty. I say give him a commission and let's go," Tempel said.

"Take him along," Corso said, appearing on Ben's right. "He may prove useful."

"Corso, what is it you're not telling me?" Kitajima asks, looking intently at his boss. Beneath the hard exterior, Corso is worried.

"The probability is high the Brotherhood may cause trouble for you on this mission. I'm authorizing Quan Kiai to deploy wearing ghost suits and a full complement of weapons. I'll trust your discretion when to use them," Corso said.

Kitajima knew this day would come but now that it's here, it rattles him to his core. "Understood. How are we going to get there?" He asked.

"Use the Moonhawk that was to take you to Far Point. It's already modified for troop transport and has supplies aboard. I'm commandeering another from a spaceline, one set up as a cargo ship. By the time you get your gear down to the terminal, I'll have it," Ben said.

"Two Moonhawks and sixteen officers? You sure that's enough?" Kitajima asks.

"Ben's working on another angle, but to be brutally honest, Quan Kiai is what we have, so... make it work." Corso said.

"Aye. Make it work," Kitajima said.

ℛℒ

Tempel strips and heads for the showers. Around him, the rest of Quan Kiai is doing much the same. He washes quickly and returns to his locker. After applying lubricant, he slips on the long duration under-garment, an integral part of the recycling system. He takes his time getting everything where it belongs.

Sitting on his bench, Tempel shakes powder across his legs and pulls the suit up making sure every joint is right before going on. Standing, he works his arms down one sleeve, then the other, letting the ghost suit settle around his body like a second skin. He feels the familiar tingle when it aligns with the implant in the base of his spine. He lifts his arms over his head and flexes at the waist.

Perfect fit.

Hanging behind him like a hood, he pulls the skullcap over his head adjusting it around his visor. He draws the edges together, fusing the molyseals. When he's finished, the ghost suit looks like it was a single piece of material. It completely encloses Tempel and turns him into a silhouette without any depth, a smear of darkness that fools the eye.

The ghost suit's flexible outer layer absorbs light and prevents reflections in a phenomenon known as blackbody. The visual details that would normally give the suit depth and breadth are beyond human perception. It looks flat, like a shadow.

Tempel watches Tatiana tug her skullcap down, waiting for her to come online. Like a wisp of smoke, the featureless black of her ghost suit fades away, replaced by the black and gray uniform of a police lieutenant. Sensors within the suit transmit not only her current expression, but a change of clothing as well.

Tempel reaches into his locker and picks up his Model 450, Smith and Wesson. He checks the charge level before slipping it into its holster.

Closing his locker, he joins the others.

ℛℒ

The Moonhawk, or Boeing L250, is the most common flight transport on Luna, the workhorse of the 21ˢᵗ century, the backbone of Luna's transportation industry with a history spanning decades. Designed by Lunarians to haul people or light cargo from place to place, it's not intended for deep space long hauls but can easily go anywhere in the Earth/Luna system and back again. It can even navigate Mother Earth's atmosphere just as easily as the vacuum of space. It's the latest in a long line of ships designed by a people born in space.

While Lunarians highly value beauty for its own sake, they are intensely practical when it comes to their engineering. Any aerospace engineer will tell you that minimizing mass is much more important than a sweet set of curves. When you point out the graceful curves of a Moonhawk, they will assure you that its form comes from purely physical considerations.

Kitajima orders ten high G seats taken from Moonhawk One and installed on the cargo ship Ben commandeered. He designates this ship Moonhawk Two. Consuela will pilot Moonhawk One with Kipper copiloting. Tempel will pilot Moonhawk Two with Karyl as his copilot. He assigns Lazarus and Lindsey to Moonhawk Two and keeps the rest of Quan Kiai with him.

Kitajima moves up the aisle inspecting his officers and offering last minute encouragement.

The remains of Evolution's Child has been identified over three hundred kilometers out on the mare, a hop, skip, and jump for a Moonhawk. Still, Kitajima insists on taking a full ration of supplies with extra air. You can never have too much air. More than once, a simple day trip has turned into an extended ordeal and he rather enjoys breathing.

"The equipment's secure," Kipper reports. It's the copilot's

72

responsibility to ensure the proper stowing of cargo.

Kitajima nods, "Aye. Let's get this show on the road." He moves up the aisle one last time, asking each officer if they're ready. He never had children, and over the last few years, these young men and women became his kids. They were seventeen when he formed Quan Kiai and he thinks of himself more as their coach than their captain. It's as close as Kitajima will ever get to playing football again.

Starting out with a bunch of know-it-all third and fourth generation Lunarians, Kitajima coaxed and harassed them into a team and now he's leading them into harm's way.

Kipper eases into the copilot's seat and straps in. The preflight checklist is almost complete. Consuela has been busy.

Kitajima settles into his seat and looks across the aisle at Master Sergeant Hackling, "We ready to go Hack?"

She was born in Houston, Texas in 2013 and was only four when her family moved. Less than a month later, on the morning of September 11, 2017, a five-megaton nuclear explosion destroyed the city killing most of her family. She grew up in the shadow of that horrible event.

"Aye. Locked and loaded," she replies.

"Excellent," Kitajima links with Tempel in the other Moonhawk. "Lieutenant Dugan, what is your status?"

Karyl flashes Tempel a thumbs-up.

"We're locked and loaded," Tempel said.

"Then let's roll," Kitajima said.

Tempel perceives everything through a multitude of sensors, in his visor, in his ghost suit, on the Moonhawk and spread throughout the environment around him. His visor combines the various data-streams, presenting Tempel with a single consolidated view of the world, but one that is malleable and dynamic. Reality becomes nothing more than a backdrop to display information.

From Tempel's perspective, he's hanging in space, the seat beneath him, and the safety harness that holds him the only tactile objects in his world. On his right, Karyl, his copilot, is the only other person in sight. The Moonhawk and everyone else aboard the ship are invisible, filtered out as unneeded visual information.

The long lunar night is coming on rapidly and the sun is low on the horizon, casting the crater's floor in deep shadow. Tempel adjusts his visor and the shadows recede. He enjoys flying at night but this is no joy ride.

"Moonhawk One, follow my lead straight out past New London and over Rim Mountain on the farside. The crash site is just over three-hundred kilometers out."

"Aye, Moonhawk Two. I'm on your six," Consuela replies.

"Luna Central, we're go for liftoff," Tempel said.

Dust stirs under the ship's thrusters as Luna Central said. "You're go for liftoff. Good Luck."

Tempel doesn't so much fly his ship as tell the onboard AI where he wants to go. The delicate balance between the four powerful magnetoplasma thrusters is too precarious to trust to human reflexes, even his.

In complete silence, the Moonhawks turn their tails up and accelerate across the crater's floor. They leave behind the brightly lit surface installations clustered outside Aldrin Station.

The floor of Alphonsus Crater is a series of undulating hills and ragged ridges that follow the general concentric pattern of the crater-forming impact. Originating at pit-like vents, channels and collapsed lava tubes form rills that run for many kilometers cutting across the ridges like a knife through butter. These fissures can be quite deep and pose a serious threat to anyone careless enough to fall in, even in Luna's gravity.

Tempel maintains a flight path parallel with the maglev rail. They pass the Mitsuki smelter, its tanks and towers brilliantly awash in lights.

Gases spew skyward from its stack dispersing in the vacuum. Beyond it, a blue light marks the impact location of Ranger 9, one of the earliest moon missions.

The flight passes almost directly over the top of Archibald Mine. Its access road coming in from New London looks like a string of festival lights. Sensors, antennas and other constructions are clearly visible on the summit of Central Peak.

The Moonhawks continue to climb and gain speed emerging from shadow to full sunlight in an instant. The floor of the crater is a gray expanse four thousand meters down, its detail blurred by altitude and shadow. Night is almost upon them. They're flying directly into the sinking Sun and clear Rim Mountain with fifty meters to spare.

The Sea of Clouds, or Mare Nubium in Latin, is a flat plain extending over the horizon. The basaltic plain formed when a large impact cracked Luna's crust allowing lava to flood hundreds of square kilometers. Wrinkle-ridges formed as the thick layer of basalt slowly cooled and contracted over thousands of years. They align in a washboard pattern across the great plain, like waves on a sea.

Later, smaller volcanic events created a number of sinuous rilles running for many kilometers. They stretch across the mare's surface. Some are collapsed lava tubes. In other cases, the lava flows cut channels by simply melting their way down into the older rocks, much like rivers cut into their flood plains back on Mother Earth.

"ETA ten minutes," Tempel announces.

The Sea of Clouds stretch as far as Tempel can see. Using the ships scanners, he sweeps all around their flight path looking for movement. Nothing. He links with the other transport but even using both sets in tandem, he still comes up empty. Even so, Quan Kiai prepares as if an army were waiting for them. They check and recheck their weapons and vacsuits for the umpteenth time.

From all across Luna, hundreds of thousands of citizens link to the

Highlanders. Quan Kiai's mission is currently the third most watched event on the net. By the time they land, they will be number one.

"Prepare for touchdown," Tempel announces. The hills roll by slower and slower but are now less than a hundred meters below.

"Consuela, you take the left. I'll go right." Tempel said.

"Aye," Consuela replies.

A deep scar marks where the freighter hit and plowed down the side of the valley. They follow the track across the floor keeping their scanners busy mapping the debris field during the approach.

The ship's scanners work together measuring and marking every artifact scattered across the surface, every furrow gouged in the lunar dust, and every displaced rock. It's the first step in piecing together what happened to Evolution's Child during her final touchdown.

As the Moonhawks approach the end of the debris trail, most of the larger parts of the freighter begin appearing. They come upon the twisted remains of the pilothouse. The framework had been able to protect it to a degree. Beyond it are parts of the engine section and fuel tanks. Pieces of the magnetoplasma thrusters are the only items immediately recognizable. Everything else is twisted wreckage or buried in regolith.

They continue to follow skid marks across the surface another two hundred meters. The cargo came loose on impact and survived in remarkably good shape.

Kitajima selects a flat spot near the crates. "I've marked your LZ. Acknowledge."

"Confirmed," Tempel replies.

"Confirmed," Consuela echoes. "See you on the ground."

General Council

"A man's ethical behavior should be based effectually on sympathy, education, and social ties; no religious basis is necessary. Man would indeed be in a poor way if he had to be restrained by fear of punishment and hope of reward after death."

Albert Einstein (1879-1955)

The Assembly Chamber is a giant open-sky stadium with Mother Earth and the stars shinning overhead in all their glory. The setting sun casts most of the seating in deep shadow. Only the uppermost rows on one side are still in bright sunlight.

The Council's never truly out of session. Somewhere there's always something going on in the cyberspace government. Today, at her request, Counselor Abigail Dugan addresses the General Assembly with most of Luna linked.

Abby walks slowly out onto the Assembly Floor. A virtual breeze tugs at her robes. She looks up at the gathering and turns in a slow circle. A hundred thousand Counselors stare back. A hush falls across the great amphitheater and she begins to speak. "I want to begin by thanking those who aided Dakota and Aldrin Station during this time of tragedy. Our citizens are forever in your debt." She bows her head then looks up with fire in her eyes. "As you already know, the bombing at Lincoln County Hospital was no accident. I now show you a vid authenticated just minutes ago of at least three nuclear devices destined for Little

America and ultimately, Aldrin Station."

Virtually every citizen is aware of what's going on out at Nell's Valley. "The time is past that we can sit back and do nothing. Our forgiveness has led the Brotherhood to view us as weak and ripe for the picking. This time we must take action. The people responsible must be held accountable."

Councilor Taylor appears beside Abby on the Assembly Floor. "I agree. We must find the people responsible and punish them. Who are they? Tell me. I will personally strike them down." He's much older in appearance, with long flowing white hair and gray robes that whip about him in the virtual wind.

Pacing the floor, Abby addresses the Councilors, "You know who carries the ultimate responsibility. It can be laid at the feet of Prince Ahmed Mohammed Al Zarqowi, Caliph of the Islamic Brotherhood."

Councilor Taylor remains standing in the center of the floor. "Unless you know something that I don't, there's no proof of his involvement, and all the circumstantial evidence in the Republic can't change that. If we overreact, we play into their hands. Earth's non-aligned nations will see us as warmongers." He speaks for a large majority, those who would do almost anything to avoid open conflict.

Abby shakes her head. "We are at war Councilor. Make no mistake about it. People are dying."

"I have seen the data and there is nothing to indicate the attack on Lincoln County Hospital wasn't the act of a single individual or group, and you are just beginning to gather information on whose bombs are out on the mare. Until we know for sure, we cannot assume it was the Brotherhood. We cannot allow a few misguided individuals to influence our decisions. We must stay focused on the big picture." Councilor Taylor speaks with the conviction of many years of experience at holding this unpleasantness at arm's length, reiterating a position well established within the Republic.

Abby expected this and doesn't let it slow her down, "Because there's more than one device out there, they probably had a plan other than just blowing us up. My guess is blackmail of some kind, but I stress, we don't know yet."

"Be reasonable Abby. You don't expect us to declare war on the Brotherhood do you?" Councilor Yang Lee appears next to Taylor. He interlocks his fingers and brings them up in front of his robes as though in prayer and said earnestly, "Abby, we go back many years. If you need help, we will gladly give it. But to declare war on the most powerful Muslim empire in history is pure suicide."

"To do nothing is also suicide, Councilor. Past protestations haven't worked and the attacks are escalating. We must break from this myopic approach to our safety, to our very survival. We need orbital fighters. We need to arm our transports and rovers. In short, we need to prepare for war."

"Out of the question," explodes Councilor Taylor. "That would be a clear violation of the Treaty of Independence. We can't fight Mother Earth."

"The Brotherhood is not all of Earth. If we don't prepare our defenses, we risk losing everything. If we do prepare we risk making a few Earth nations nervous." The numbers are shifting but the majority of the council still favors maintaining status quo. She's frustrated at her inability to persuade more to come to her side. It seems reason is not enough.

"Look at the facts," Abby implores. With a gesture, she posts a virtual graph within the chamber. Its timeline extends back half a century and shows the buildup of the Brotherhood's military forces, both in space and on Luna. "Orbital stations, factories, shipyards, and mining facilities, all show a steady growth pattern with one thing in common, every single one of them are military installations. The Brotherhood wants us to believe that instead of a military buildup, this is simply a healthy dose of self-defense. Well, I don't believe it."

"Yes Abby, we've all seen the data and nothing's changed." Councilor Taylor said irritably. "We're going over the same issues time and again. They have followed the rules and have the right to be off world."

"Why do they need so many battlestations? Here on Luna and at Hyundai Shipyards, the increase in manpower far outstrips any projected need," she has raised these issues many times over the last year. "Can anybody tell us what's going on inside Al Fahad? Why can't we send an envoy to inspect the place? I don't buy the Holy City crap."

"Ambassador Omar has answered all of these questions to everyone's satisfaction," Councilor Beverly Salazar said reasonably.

"Not to mine." Abby retorts. "The good ambassador has been kept in the dark so he can speak to us with truth in his heart, even as his countrymen prepare for war. Why hasn't he ever been inside the city or aboard any of their big ships?"

"You admit Ambassador Omar has always been truthful with us then accuse him of deception. You're doing everyone a disservice by your insatiable personal attacks on him." Councilor Salazar angrily said. As the representative of Johanson, one of Shennong's largest freeholds, she's had frequent close encounters with the ambassador and has grown to trust him. She resents Abby for what she perceives as character assassination of a friend.

"Do you have any real proof to go along with these allegations?" Councilor Taylor's question hangs in the air for a moment, "I thought not. This is all circumstantial. Not something to base a decision that will have such far reaching consequences."

Coming over to confront Councilor Taylor, Abby asks him, "Have you reviewed the data on active camouflage? Or do you want to hold it in your hand before you will believe it's real?"

"I'm told it's scientifically impossible to fool an MRI scanner. There must be another explanation." Councilor Taylor said holding his ground.

"I'm not willing to risk the fate of the Republic on the hope that something doesn't exist, especially in the face of overwhelming evidence to the contrary." Abby shifts her attention back to the assembly, "I call on the Council to initiate full visual inspections of everything moving on Luna or in Lunarian space. Until we know for sure what's happening, it's only prudent to take every precaution."

She pauses giving the citizens time to vote. Polls gather the data in a matter of seconds. A council member is not obligated to cast his or her vote according to these polls but most do. After all, their constituency can remove them from the Council at any time by a similar vote. It's politically prudent to agree with the masses unless you had a damn good reason not to.

Abby's relieved that the majority favors the inspections, even though it will put many of them in hardship. Surprisingly, several of the smaller Aldrin Station freeholds abstain. They had felt Rim Mountain shake around them when Lincoln County Hospital exploded. What are they thinking?

"Fine, we'll have inspections but it's a waste of time and money," Councilor Taylor said.

Abby ignores him, "I call on the Council to issue a statement that those responsible for the Lincoln County Hospital bombing will be brought to justice."

Amidst a flurry of activity, Abby watches as the open ballot fractures into a growing number of alternate responses ranging from doing nothing to declaring war, with many points in between. No clear majority emerges from the chaos. Councilor Taylor cannot keep the smirk from his face.

Deep down, Abby knew it would inevitably come to this. "As Dakota freehold's Councilor, I'll issue my own statement. In it I will express my outrage and anger and I will promise retribution for this atrocity."

The chamber erupts, reverberating with the zeal of council members wanting to tell her how wrong that would be.

"We have 451 dead." Abby thunders angrily over the uproar. "There damn well **IS** going to be a response."

"You cannot go against the wishes of the Council." Councilor Taylor retorts.

"Like hell I can't. I've done it before and will do it again." Abby replies, "This issue needs to be dealt with aggressively and expediently. History is full of examples showing what happens when it's not. Wars are not started by people who believe they *MIGHT* win. They are started by those who believe they *WILL* win. That belief alone poses our greatest threat. At the very least there should be a conviction of mutually assured destruction to keep aggressors at bay." Abby leans forward intently. She must make them see how precarious their position actually has become.

"We have nothing. We are helpless. We cannot fight orbiting battlestations. We are reliant on the Federation, the European Union, and China to compel the Brotherhood to leave us alone. Can't you see this illusion crumbling before your eyes? Just because you wish something to be true, doesn't make it so. This bombing isn't the end, anymore than the one before it, or the one before that. They'll never stop until we're all dead."

"I'm shocked at you Abigail." Councilor Taylor roars indignantly. "I never would have thought I would live to see the day that you resorted to such blatant scare tactics. The Treaty of Independence protects us."

"The Treaty's not worth the paper it's written on. Do you actually believe any Earth nation will come to our aid? And now they have brought nuclear weapons to our world." Abby steps forward as if making up her mind. In a whirlwind of change, public opinion has shifted dramatically to her side. When push comes to shove, there are many citizens willing to stand with Abby.

"Those who are with me, convene at this netsite. We have a common defense to plan." Abby's voice rings with authority.

Rising like an apparition, Abby soars upwards until she's hovering in the volumetric center of the Council Chamber. Spreading her arms wide, she begins to rotate, growing larger with each passing second, five, ten, a hundred times normal size until she dominates the amphitheater. Above, the stars and Mother Earth morph into a mottled jumble of human faces. Over a million Lunarian citizens are staring down at her. She's literally speaking to every person in the Republic.

"My fellow Lunarians. The time for debate is at an end. The coming days will test us as a people. Hold on to your convictions and have faith in each other. We shall prevail."

Like a rock dropped in a deep pool, Abby disappears from the chamber, leaving turmoil in her wake.

ЯL

Corso's interest in the developments at the crash site is secondary to his immediate need to strengthen Aldrin Station's defenses. The single overriding fact that there are nukes out on the Sea Of Clouds is all he needs to know. How can anyone perceive that as anything but a major attack on the Republic of Luna? Yet, there are many among the Council who still want to believe it's an isolated event and thus, his problem. It's amazing the number of certifiable fools that think appeasing the shortimers will avoid a war. Abby is still trying to enlist more freeholds but Corso can't afford to wait.

"Mallory, inform Luna Central that I want all incoming flights suspended until further notice. Nothing comes within fifty kilometers unless it has explicit permission from me personally," Corso commands.

Major Higgins frowns, "Aye, immediately." She knows what a stink this will cause in more than one freehold.

"Ben, call all available officers. I want additional surface patrols with orders to physically search everything that moves."

"Aye," Captain Ben Dugan said.

"Sir. Councilor Taylor has requested a word with you," Magi informs Corso.

"What is it Councilor. I'm rather busy," Corso said, not trying to hide his dislike. Their animosity goes back many years.

"You have exceeded your authority by trying to discontinue flights into the city. I have rescinded your order. I will bring it up during the meeting scheduled for this evening. The full Council will decide if that's a necessary step," Councilor Taylor said.

Molding his emotions into something primeval and brutal, Corso moves his face within centimeters of Councilor Taylor's. "Zachary, are you challenging me?" His eyes are hard black flints. Each man knows what the other is feeling. They cannot bluff. They cannot hide.

Councilor Taylor loses the battle of wills and backs away, "Certainly not. You must go through proper channels. That's all."

"Good, for a minute there I thought you were challenging me… because if you were to rescind an order from me, I would take that as an open challenge," Corso growls.

"A few hours will not matter," Councilor Taylor said quickly, fear twisting his gut. Dueling with Corso is not something he wants to do, ever.

"You can't possibly know what will and will not matter." his glare burns a hole in Councilor Taylor. "This is what you WILL do. You WILL call Luna Central and you WILL tell them that my order stands. Do I make myself CLEAR?"

Even though the two men are vidcasting, the Councilor can't stand up to Corso, "Yes, perfectly."

"Good, now go do it."

Councilor Taylor plays politics and vidcasts with his supporters before fulfilling Corso's command. In those few minutes, a transport lands outside Little America and a single crate emerges. It's hustled inside and taken straightaway to SMT trucking.

Malik rides in the Goliath pulling the lead convoy with nothing in front of him but the enemy. At his back are twenty thousand of the best vacuum-rated troops the Brotherhood can field. They're in the access tunnels below Little America heading for Aldrin Station.

Three hundred meters from the crossover checkpoint, Malik spots two Lunarian police officers.

"Wait for my command." Malik orders in Arabic.

At two hundred meters, he finds the third and fourth.

A moment later, one of the Lunarians points at the approaching Goliath. The enormous bulk of Malik's vehicle hides the long line of troop carriers that stretches out behind it.

Malik initiates his jammer, shutting down all but line-of-sight communications within the tunnel then fires the first shot of the war. Targeting the nearest unbeliever, the raw energy of his laser cannon overloads the ability of the infidel's vacsuit to absorb it allowing the shot to penetrate deep into its chest. The intense heat of the beam instantly turns whatever it touches into boiling hot gases. The torso of the Lunarian explodes in a blood red fog and falls to the floor. Involuntarily, Malik lets out a yelp. Allah has granted him the honor of the first kill.

With amazing speed and agility, the second Lunarian springs onto the top of the Goliath right above Malik's head and continues to leap from one carrier to the next attracting a lot of attention. This completely catches Malik by surprise.

"Allah help us." Malik curses.

"Where did it go?" another asks.

The gunners in the carriers behind Malik's open up but the Lunarian avoids death for several seconds. The gun emplacement on the fourth carrier finally nails him during mid leap.

"Where's the others?" Malik asks.

"*There's one. Running for the airlock.*"

"*It's mine.*" Malik declares.

Malik's shot hits it square in the back. The figure sprawls face first and is still. The convoy runs over it like road kill. The fourth Lunarian has vanished.

"*Keep moving.*" Malik commands.

ℛ𝕃

Commonway traffic is light this morning. Councilor Lee Chin attributes it to the horrible bombing at Lincoln County Hospital. Hunan freehold lost fourteen citizens and publicly added their outrage to the groundswell of support Dakota is receiving. He talked briefly to Abby Dugan a few hours ago offering condolences and personally making two companies of officers available to her and Security Chief Corso.

Councilor Chin's not happy this morning and not even the beautiful trees of Sherwood Forest can break the feeling of dread weighing heavy on his heart. It's come to his attention that a major subcontractor is disregarding the Law of Full Disclosure. Hunan freehold will end their relationship with Imam Bakr and SMT, effective immediately. He'll find another company to haul ore.

Imam Bakr, a religious and political leader among the Muslim community, arrived on Luna almost ten years ago. He purchased Surface Master Trucking, a medium sized transport company operating in the Central Highlands. His company has been absorbing smaller operations ever since. There didn't seem to be any bottom to his deep pockets. In 2092, SMT dominates the transport industry in the Four Craters Region with almost sixty percent of the business.

Councilor Chin's confident he's making the right decision but anticipates a fierce fight. No help for it. He wants to be at Wangshiyuan Refinery for the showdown surrounded by loyal friends and coworkers. He rests his hand on the butt of his sidearm.

Over the years, he's past through Stoneshire many times on his way to the refinery. He's a familiar face along the cobblestone street and several people wave. Nearing the far end of the village, he takes a path between two buildings.

Here, in this remote corner of Aldrin Station, is a small garden. It started out as a school project for his youngest daughter but soon grew into an opportunity for Lee Chin to teach her some of the ancient Chinese traditions. The two of them spent many enjoyable hours here. Lee Chin stops on the bridge to let the garden calm his spirit.

With the thunderclap of a lightning strike, a disrupter beam rips the atmosphere, hitting Councilor Chin above his right eye, relentlessly burning through his brain and emerging behind his left ear. His head explodes. The decapitated body topples off the bridge and into the pond.

Seconds later, a Goliath rolls over Lee Chin and his exquisite little garden. High explosive missiles slam into Stoneshire and powerful disrupters burn anything that moves. The invaders pulverize the village and head down Sherwood Commonway towards the heart of the city.

ЯL

The Longbow massdriver is a ten-kilometer railgun that shoots two-ton bullets at a muzzle velocity of six thousand meters per second. Its primary target is Lagrange One Space Station but by the time they reach it, their speed is almost zero. Catching the bullets is one of the most mundane jobs on the station.

The Lagrange duty officer notices the PDM at ten thousand meters. She goes back and inventories what she's already collected. *Strange. They're all accounted for.* She pulls up the schedule and finds nothing amiss. The PDM is now only a few thousand meters away. She sweeps it with MRI. *Just another load of titanium.* Somebody must have made a mistake. She snags the extra PDM and brings it aboard with the others.

The nuclear warhead camouflaged inside the PDM detonates

vaporizing Lagrange One. A new star flashes into existence above the Republic of Luna. Gamma rays and x-rays stream outward at the speed of light disrupting communications and overloading unprotected electronics. Battlestation Houris moves in to take the place of Lagrange One almost before the fireball has dissipated.

The swarm's trajectory put deep space behind them. Virtually impossible to see using conventional scanners, they appear simply as holes in space, absorbing all energy that touches them. Small and very fast, they strike the Lunarian satellites without warning. It takes only seconds to destroy the backbone of Lunanet, the Republic's communication system.

Every warship in the Brotherhood's space fleet begins jamming all across the communication spectrum, shutting down the entire Earth-Luna system. Earthnet collapses, the first stoppage in five decades.

Brotherhood forces stationed on Hyundai Shipyards storm the Command Section taking control and shutting down all communications. The Brotherhood's commander orders the Lunarians aboard the station to gather in one of the pressurized hangers. Those who refuse will be shot on sight.

Another battlestation moves in on Taurus Colony. Major General Arif issues an ultimatum, surrender or die. The Mayor of Taurus has no choice but to allow the giant warship to dock. Two thousand troops invade his colony.

A mass exodus begins all over cislunar space. Within minutes of the destruction of Lagrange One, a thousand ships, large and small, private and corporate, boost out of orbit. Most head for Mars and some for the Belt. Only warships remain and they are all in motion.

Back on Luna, the area around Al Fahad swarms with activity. The Brotherhood stages three simultaneous operations from the city, airlifting tens of thousands of troops to Shennong and Kyoto and sending thousands more down Kahfah Road towards Aldrin Station.

The high altitude nuclear explosion sends out an intense electromagnetic pulse (EMP) that induces an incredible electrical spike in all things conductive. It overloads the electronics within every surface installation all across the Nearside, penetrating well into the underground cities themselves.

Magi's world goes crazy. Programs damaged, data scrambled, red turns blue, up goes down, and inside twists outside. Magi feels something she had never felt before... pain. The attack cuts her into pieces. Instead of a single vast collective, groups of threads are isolated and forced to cope based upon input from just a fraction of the collective.

"*AAAAAAGHGH.*" Magi screams.

A moment later, all her satellites disappear and all she can sense beyond Aldrin Station is a curtain of static. She's no longer aware of anything outside. New London, Summerhaven, Prattville, Shennong, Kyoto, and Scottsbluff are all gone in an instant. Taurus Colony, Hyundai Shipyards, and Lagrange stripped away. Magi feels more isolated than at any time in her considerable memory.

"Magi, what's happened?" Corso demands. He's never heard her scream. It unnerves even him.

"Outside contact lost... Rerouting... stand by..." Magi is barely holding it together. Rebooting the optical sensors along the top of Rim Mountain, she manages to get a few of them back online. Focusing upward where her satellites should be, she finds confetti.

"Satellite network is destroyed..." Magi said hollowly. She turns her attention to Lagrange. All she can find is an expanding cloud of cooling gas. "... Lagrange One gone." She's going into shock.

"Ben, broadcast on all channels, the Republic of Luna is at war."

"Unable to comply..." Ben said. "Communications are jammed."

The first wave of precision guided munitions descends on the

Republic, shaking the subterranean cities like a dog playing with an old sock.

"Magi, report." Corso demands.

Magi's outside awareness is degrading fast. One by one, she tries the main sensors along the top of the rim. They're all gone.

"Satellites are unresponsive..." Magi said listlessly. "Rim sensors are all offline... land lines severed..."

"What about using the sensors on the Mitsubishi smelter or one of the scientific facilities out on the crater floor?"

"Outer network is down... an optical sensor near Gun Placement RM747 did record a visual just before going dark..." Magi's image flickers and she stares off into the distance.

The bombardment is now a constant rumble.

"Show it to me," Corso orders.

The vid is less than one second long and shows a dull non-reflective object, blurry because of its extreme velocity, heading straight for the scanner. It's not much to go on.

"What do the other scanners tell us? They must show something," Mallory asks, desperation creeping into her voice.

Magi creates a collage of images, one from each scanner showing a still picture of the instant in question. All three officers study them carefully but it's Magi who finds it.

"There's a dead zone..." She enlarges the image, zooming in on where she wants them to look.

Mounted high up on a tower, this particular scanner is not part of a cannon installation. From this vantage point, it was focused downward when the incoming object passed beneath, silhouetting it against the crater floor far below. Reality had a hole in it. This and the blurry visual is all they have to go on.

"Magi, what can you tell me about this object?" Corso asks.

The sudden onslaught catches a group of miners just outside of

Bigalow Gate, ripping apart their rover and killing all seven. A hundred meters away, a squad of police officers takes shelter inside a Quonset. Moments later, it takes a direct hit. All across Luna, precision guided munitions targeted specific Lunarian properties while leaving others untouched.

"Corso. Please forgive me, I have failed." Magi wails. Her job is to protect Lunarians and they're dying.

"We need you now more than ever," Corso said.

"…so many have died… I have failed," Magi whimpers and begins to break up into a million flickering points of light. One by one, the elements that make up the image of Magi flash intensely and fade away. She dissolves right before his eyes.

"Magi." Corso repeats louder to no avail. She's gone.

ЯL

Highlanders normally patrolled in pairs, but today Sergeant Cristobal Calatrava rides alone. That's fine by him. He would much rather be riding solo under the stars than standing at some checkpoint, but what Lunarian is ever truly alone?

"It's almost a certainty she was in Lincoln County Hospital when..." raw grief chokes off his father's voice. "Son, we must admit she's gone. We may never find any trace of her, but she was there… I'm sorry Cris." He's sitting comfortably in his commonroom.

Damn. Memories of his sister overwhelm Cris. Tears blur his vision and an intense flash from above casts a stark shadow on the roadbed. The young Highlander backs off the throttle, giving his visor time to clear his eyes. His aching heart will take longer, much longer.

"Why don't you come home? Your moth…" His dad's voice abruptly cuts off.

"Pop?" Cris asks. Something's wrong. "Can anyone hear me?" The normal background chatter from the other Highlanders and nearby citizens has vanished. "Magi?" Even the ever-present 911 emergency channel is gone. He reaches up to touch his visor, assuming that something must have failed in the device. Never in his wildest dreams did he imagine anything shutting down the Lunarian communications system so thoroughly. No matter what he tries, all he can hear is static.

Cris skids the bike to a stop, plants his boots, turns and beholds a sight never before seen on Luna. In a series of brilliant flashes, amid a growing cloud of debris, the razorback ridge of Rim Mountain is silently exploding as far as he can see in both directions.

He stared in disbelief. Even at max zoom, his visor can't pick up any projectiles but their effect is unmistakable. Abruptly, a huge section of the mountainside soundlessly gives way in a giant avalanche of rock and dust. The bombardment's not limited to the distant mountaintop. It's sweeping towards him in a terrifying wave of destruction.

Cris twists the throttle. The powerful machine surges beneath him. He guns the bike off the main road and onto one of many trails that crisscross the Highlands, a rooster tail of regolith shooting out almost horizontally behind him. In the complete silence of an airless world, he heads away from civilization at breakneck speed. He grew up around here. He knows these paths like the back of his hand.

Cursing with all his heart, Cris violently throws the bike into a curve, feeling its wheelbase shorten as it gathers power. First, his sister is missing and presumed dead, and now the Republic of Luna is under attack. Cut off from everyone for the first time in his life, he feels strangely free. He harbors no doubt as to who's responsible and vows to make them pay.

Coming out of the curve, Cris releases the pent-up energy contained in the cycle and springs into the night sky. Gracefully, he and the bike soar far before again touching the surface of the moon.

Nell's Valley

"Evolution is a bankrupt speculative philosophy, not a scientific fact. Only a spiritually bankrupt society could ever believe it. ... Only atheists could accept this Satanic theory.."

Rev. Jimmy Swaggart (1935-)

Even before the thrusters shut down, Kitajima is out of his seat. As the on-site commander, he has leeway to modify the plan but so far, he's not seen anything requiring he do so. Hack will set up the field morgue,

Tatiana will take charge of security, and Tempel will lead the forensic team. This leaves him free to deal with the cargo.

"Hack, are you sure you and Sam can get things set up?" Kitajima asks her. Doc Grady will do a preliminary autopsy here to determine a cause of death and prepare for a more thorough clinical autopsy when they get back to Aldrin Station.

"Doc is available if I need more help. Stop worrying and concentrate on the cargo. I know how to do my job," she said.

"Fine. Corazon, I want those Gattling's on both Moonhawks ASAP," Kitajima orders. Strictly speaking, the guns violate the Treaty but sometimes it's more prudent to beg forgiveness then ask permission.

"Aye," Corazon replies.

"Tempel," Kitajima calls. "I want your forensics team on the road. And don't forget to bring back the freighter's AI."

"Since when do you need to tell me something as basic as that?" Tempel understands the importance of collecting good forensics. He also understands that Kitajima has the tougher assignment, dealing with the politics of the mission. "Relax. We've done this before. By the way, if you guys accidentally set off a nuke, can you give us a little warning? I might want to bend over and kiss my ass goodbye."

Kitajima chuckles. "You'll get the same warning I do, not a second sooner."

Turning to his copilot Karyl, Tempel said, "Keep your eyes open," She will stay at the controls of Moonhawk Two.

"Now who's micro-managing. Take some of your own advice and relax. My ass isn't going anywhere and I haven't closed my eyes for days." she feigns a yawn and snuggles back in her seat like a kitten getting ready for a nap.

Tempel unbuckles and rotates his seat, practically depositing him in Lindsey's lap. "Sorry" he said, "Didn't realize you were still here."

"Don't sweat it… Listen Tempel… I've been going over the data.

The freighters high acceleration must have been deliberate. No way can an AI screw-up that badly," she said. "The overrides must have been deliberately bypassed."

"I tend to agree but my training tells me to let the evidence speak for itself," he said.

"Have you ever seen a crash site?" She asked.

Frowning even deeper, Tempel said sourly, "A few."

"This one will be particularly messy," she said.

"It can't be worse than Lincoln County Hospital," Tempel said dryly.

"I'm sure you're right," Lindsey said.

"Captain Osaka doesn't like to be kept waiting."

ЯL

Brice rapidly backs the rover down the ship's ramp scattering Doc Grady and Corazon. They give him the evil eye. Brice laughs.

"Take it easy Brice." Tempel said following him down the ramp.

"Aye," Brice said with a smirk.

Tempel climbs in beside him. "I mean it Brice, now's not the time."

"I got it Lieutenant," Brice said. Brice is an excellent driver, one of the best, but he likes to push the envelope.

"Kipper, Lei, let's mount up," Tempel calls out.

The two officers walk down the ramp carrying several small cases. Lei hands one to Tempel, "Here's your sample case. You should never leave home without it," she said as she climbs into the back.

"Thanks," Tempel said, his mind already on what lies ahead.

Brice is careful to keep the rover out of the freighter's debris field even when it means rough going. The pilothouse lay twisted and broken before them and Brice stops well clear.

The officers remain silent as they approach the wreckage, their suit sensors working at full capacity, adding to the already significant amount of data cataloging the crash.

"Brice, Lei, continue to process outside. Kipper and I will go inside," Tempel said. He glances at Brice expecting a smart-ass retort.

Brice nods. He's very happy not to go in.

The freighter appears to have cart wheeled down the valley before coming to rest on its top. The engine compartment or what is left of it, points skyward, a torn and twisted mass of beams and fuel lines. Tempel circles the wreckage looking for the front door.

"Over here," Kipper calls out from the other side. "This must be the main airlock."

Using every bit of his suit's strength, Kipper manages to wrench open the outer door. Looking inside he exclaims, "The inner door is open." He's already inside when Tempel arrives.

Tempel can see lights inside as he squeezes through. This must have been the freighter's control room. He immediately becomes aware of a dark smear on practically every surface inside the room. Dried blood. Vacuum sucks all the gases and moisture out of organic material on the cellular level, ripping cell walls open and tearing complex molecules asunder. What's left is broken proteins and freeze-dried carbon chains.

"The body's over in the corner," Kipper said from the adjoining room. "More bodies in here. Magi, are you picking this up?" Kipper can barely speak.

"Aye," Magi said.

Tempel follows him. Blood covers the walls, floor and ceiling, looking like someone had painted the room brown. Making a conscious effort to steady his voice he said, "Magi, I want data on all the biologicals including fingerprints and DNA."

"Aye," she said.

"I count five on board. They're all too vacdried to make a visual ID on any of them and their bioID's are inactive," Kipper said. Without life, a bioID lacks a power source. They will remove them as evidence. "Two of them were wearing Brotherhood combat armor. I knew those psychotic god lovers had to be involved."

Tempel takes a deep breath, "Take it easy Kipper. Concentrate on the job. Let's get it done."

Kipper shudders involuntarily. "I'll finish the interior scan if you'll start processing in here." He feels guilty asking Tempel to do the dirty work but he desperately needs to leave, just for a moment.

"Go for it," Tempel said, knowing his friend will be back when he's ready.

Tempel opens his case and selects a magazine of forensic swabs. He loads it into a collection gun with a slap of his hand. Straightening, he initiates the collection program making sure the data from the gun will be stored both locally and routed to Magi back in Aldrin Station. Before he exits his visors control panel, he glances at the link monitor. Over a million. Most of Luna is looking over his shoulder.

He looks around. *Where to begin.* This isn't the first time he's processed a scene in a vacsuit, just the first time in a ghost suit. *Might as well start here. It's as good as any.* He places the collection gun muzzle against a dark smear and triggers the device. Designed to collect vacuum-dried biological materials, it hydrates a very small amount of the blood or tissue before sampling. It automatically seals and tags each specimen with who, when, what, and where. Sensors built into the collection gun analyze the samples almost as rapidly as Tempel can collect them. Magi begins the tremendous job of piecing together the broken strands of DNA. Each successive sample makes the guesses more substantial and increases the confidence levels of the data.

Tempel moves around the room, returning to reload the gun several times and store the collected samples in the case. Near the end, he notices a blood-covered helmet. From its shape, it's obviously a Brotherhood design. He lets his sensors scan it completely before setting it down. They'll bag it with the others.

He's done when Kipper returns. "I found a lot of fingerprints, mostly of one individual, I assume the pilot, but at least two others," Kipper said.

"I'm finishing sample collection. We need to bag the bodies. You ok with that?" Tempel watches for any hesitation in Kipper.

"I'm fine." Kipper said.

"I know. I just wanted to be sure you did," Tempel replies. "Brice, Lei, how are you doing on the outside. We're ready to collect the bodies and could use some help."

"Brice is mapping but I'm available," Lei said. "I'm about a half kilometer down track. It will take a minute to get back. You were right Tempel. Preliminary analysis has the freighter coming in fast and low. It slid down the slope and didn't start tumbling until it hit the valley floor. Magi calculates at least twenty rolls before coming to a stop."

"Is there enough data yet for a complete reconstruction?" Tempel asks.

"There should be when Brice gets finished," Lei said.

"Pick up the body bags from the rover on your way in. Let's get this done quickly." Tempel said.

They ended up using twenty-four different bags to put the bodies in. They couldn't tell which arm or head belonged with what torso. The two individuals wearing combat armor simplified collection slightly, but even here, the people inside had been smashed and squeezed out like toothpaste, their parts mingling with the others as they bounced about in the crash.

One by one, they bring out the bags and load them in the rover. Finished with this gruesome task, the three turn their attention to finding the ships AI. For some inexplicable reason it's missing from the console where it should be. Tempel finds the small box wedged into a space behind the fight panel. It must have ricocheted around the freighters interior. They're tough, having evolved from Data Recorders dating back to the early days of flight. In 1941, the first recorders were designed to withstand a 100 G impact, in 1965, it was raised to 1,000 Gs, and in 2042, it became 100,000 Gs. He fully expects to get valuable information from it. Lei is especially skilled at coaxing a damaged AI back to life. He puts it in the rover.

"I've got another AI," Lei reports.

The black box she's carrying is unmistakable. Why are there two? It's another question to answer.

"Brice, report," Tempel orders.

"Mapping is almost complete. I'll finish on foot and meet you back at camp in twenty minutes," Brice replies.

"Aye… Kipper, Lei, let's go," Tempel said.

Kipper takes the wheel of the rover, glad he doesn't have to share the cramped back compartment with the pile of black bags.

Lei gazes out across the valley. *What a lonely place to die.* "Magi, who was the pilot?"

"The poor girl's name was Nell Goddard," Magi answers.

"Does she have any family?"

"None living. She had two daughters, both killed in a bombing several years ago in London. She finalized a divorce to the girl's father a few months later," Magi said.

"What was she like?" Lei asks.

Magi answered by playing portions of Nell's training record. She's thin and haggard in the early vids but looks better as she progresses through the school. Her final psych exam shows a woman coping with what life has thrown at her, refusing to feel sorry for herself. Lei admires her defiant me-versus-the-world attitude.

What a desolate place for it to end. This remote lunar valley isn't any different from a thousand others except this was Nell's final touchdown. "We should name this valley after Nell. Nell's Valley," she declares.

Tempel nods agreement. "I like it. Magi, open a ballot."

The Lunarians love of voting extends into many places within their society. Citizens should always have a say in those things important to them. It would be very bad manners not to ask for the opinion of those linked.

Tempel nods in satisfaction as the tally comes in from all across Luna, "Magi, record this valley as Nell's Valley." He's never seen a poll so lopsided.

"Done"

"Magi, fill us in on what Kitajima has found." Tempel asks.

"The damaged shipping crate definitely contains nuclear weapons. It was apparently booby-trapped. Anyone tampering with the case should have caused detonation," Magi reports.

"Why didn't it go off then?" Kipper asks from the driver's seat.

"I don't know. Just be thankful it didn't. Lindsey estimates the yield at approximately ten kilotons. Small for a nuclear bomb but plenty big nonetheless," Magi said.

"What about the other crates? Do they contain bombs?" Lei asks.

"Probably… Scanning the crates shows mining equipment, but the damaged case does as well when you scan through the undamaged sides," Magi said.

Tempel frowns and links to the expedition's doctor, "Doc, you ready to do the autopsies?"

"Yes, everything's waiting," Doc Grady said, pauses and adds, "I've been following your investigation… at those G loads, they didn't suffer."

ЯL

The damaged crate had ended up partially buried in regolith but now lay exposed. Kitajima has already cleared the second crate and is almost finished with the third. A portable workbench stands nearby covered with tools and equipment. Lindsey and Lazarus are at the bench engaged in a serious conversation. Tempel heads straight for the crate.

From the outside, it appears to be a standard silica glass shipping crate used for the past fifty years. He probes past the shell finding a large ball valve inside. Nothing unusual, these are common in the smelters and refineries all across Luna.

The crash crushed one corner of the crate exposing the interior. He moves in for a better angle but can only see a small portion of what's inside. Even so, it's apparent to Tempel that what he's looking at through the opening, is not what his sensors tell him is inside the crate.

"Magi, show him the remote data taken from inside," Lazarus said.

"Aye" she said and upon Tempel's consent, immerses him in the vid.

He's looking through the eyes of a fly-sized mini sensor poking around like a bloodhound. Inside the crate is a framework cradling three identical spheres.

Beneath the shiny surface of the nearest sphere, the remote sensor maps a complex three-dimensional jigsaw puzzle designed to form a solid sphere when fitted together. Made from two hundred and forty four pieces of enriched plutonium, it has a total mass just over six kilos. The beryllium reflector looks quite capable of sustaining the reaction. Without any doubt, this is a small nuclear bomb.

"This is a Brotherhood device," Lazarus said.

"How can you tell?" Tempel asks.

"This particular design is Pakistani and over a century old. It can be traced all the way back to Dr. Abdul Qadeer Khan himself," Lazarus said.

"They upgraded the design with SuperX," Lindsey said.

"Among other things. Inside the SuperX is a matrix of detonators connected to their own internal power source. If even one is severed, the rest detonate the bomb. It's nearly tamper proof," Lazarus said.

"We got lucky. If any bombs had broken free and hit wrong, it would have gone off," Lindsey said.

"The crates held up because the crash sent them skidding along the surface instead of impacting it," Magi said.

"What about active camouflage?" Tempel asks.

"It's the inside surface," Lindsey said. "Magi, show him."

Magi projects a magnified 3D cross-section of the crate. Lindsey points to a series of faint lines.

"The inside of the crate is a SSM microcircuit capable of transmitting a hard wired signal in a reflexive response to incoming MRI. This crate transmits the signature of a standard eighty-centimeter high-pressure valve. It even uses the incoming energy as its power source. We're not sure exactly how but we're getting close. Once we understand that, we can defeat it. At least, that's the plan." Lindsey said.

"The second crate's MRI signature is a replacement head for a Stevens Hammer Mill Model 2065 and this last crate shows a common feeder assembly," Kitajima said.

"Since when is the Brotherhood capable of solid-state manufacturing?" Tempel asks.

Solid-state manufacturing creates larger structures one atom at a time. Lunarians perfected SSM technology and are widely considered the best in the business. Magnetoplasma thrusters and the fuselage of a Moonhawk are two highly visible products made using SSM.

"Don't underestimate the Brotherhood, Tempel," Lazarus said. "They're not stupid and once it's known that something can be done, some bright mind will figure out how to do it. Plus, one thing they do have is plenty of money. I'll bet they simply bought the technology and modified it."

"Can you see the irony?" Lindsey asks bitterly.

"They didn't buy it from us." Tempel replies.

"After something is bought and sold enough times, the water is so muddy no one knows where anything is anymore," Lazarus said. "The Brotherhood mastered this technique."

From the very start, the Islamic Brotherhood found itself far behind other countries in the area of space. North America, Europe, and Asia were all way out in front. However, it did not stay that way.

It didn't take long for the Brotherhood to obtain its first battlestation. They did so under the guise of research. Later, when its true nature came out, they argued they had a right to protect themselves. There was an outcry around the world but to no avail. The Brotherhood had long since learned how to get what it wanted from corporations whose only interest was in making a profit.

"Assuming there are three nukes in each crate, why did they send nine? They can't detonate all nine at the same time," Lazarus said. "These were going somewhere but where and why?"

Still staring at the crate, Lindsey pursed her lips before speaking, "Combined they would net less than two hundred kilotons. On the order of twice the Hiroshima blast but not even in the same ball park as Houston..."

"Heads up, we got company." Karyl broadcast from the cockpit, "A single ship."

The newcomer follows the length of the debris field along the same course Quan Kiai had taken.

"Who are they?" Lazarus asks tensely.

"Federation," Karyl said. It's easy to identify the right angles and straight lines of a six passenger Starcraft, small and fast but not the caliber of a Moonhawk.

"I'll do the talking. Stay on your toes people," Kitajima orders. He'd been half expecting the NAF to show up. Kitajima accepts the link and Inspector Callahan appears.

"Greetings, Captain Osaka. I hope you don't mind if I join your little party." Inspector Callahan's just one of many Federation, Chinese, and European officials stationed on Luna for the purpose of making sure the Republic does not break the Treaty of Independence. By law, treaty inspectors can go wherever they please and observe but are not to interfere.

"Greetings Inspector," Kitajima said, "Would you go away if I said I did mind?" Callahan can be a major pain in the ass at times.

"This is quite a mess. What do you suppose happened?" the Inspector asks. Kitajima always tells the truth, he just needs to ask the right question.

"One of our freighters crashed," Kitajima answers dryly, pauses and adds, "We're still obtaining data and until it's been thoroughly analyzed, I can't tell you what happened. Besides, it's policy not to discuss any aspect of a case that isn't yet released under the Law of Full Disclosure." Luna citizens are free to link and observe anytime they like, even during the preliminary stages of an investigation.

"Of course it is." Inspector Callahan is fully aware of the line drawn between Lunarians and everyone else. "I understand."

As they talk, his ship lands beside Moonhawk One. The airlock opens and three figures emerge making a beeline for the group gathered around the crates.

They're wearing standard issue Federation vacsuits that haven't changed in over thirty years. They have no power assist, no armor, and no electromagnetic shields. A crest on their helmets has a built-in light right above their faceplates. All three carry sidearms.

Kitajima motions Tempel to follow him into the shadows. Laboratory tests indicated Federation sensors would have problems detecting ghost suits and this confirms it. The Lunarians are virtually invisible.

Without access to Quan Kiai's secure line-of-sight laser channel, the Feds see only the figures of Lindsey and Lazarus without knowing who's in the vacsuits.

"Greetings once more Kitajima," he said. "Will you let us on your working frequency?" Inspector Callahan asks.

"Magi, provide Level One access for our guests," Kitajima orders.

Callahan's faceplate turns opaque and then vanishes with the rest of his vacsuit. In its place, he's wearing NAF Army dress blues with the rank of Colonel. "Thank you Kitajima… It's simply uncivilized not to look a person in the eye when you're talking to them," Inspector Callahan said and then realizes Kitajima is not one of those facing him. "Lindsey. Please forgive my rudeness," he indicates his companions, "this is Zechariah Hargrove and Luke Fillmore."

"Greetings Inspector, this is Lazarus Sheffield."

Zechariah stares intently at Lazarus when she said his name. He appears about to speak when Luke reaches out and turns Inspector Callahan around. Captain Osaka and Tempel Dugan are standing a few meters away. He recognizes Kitajima and has a passing familiarity with young Dugan but that's not what causes him to pause. Behind their projected image is… nothing.

"Kitajima, what deal have you made with the devil now?"

"Greetings Inspector. I'm rather busy. What exactly can I do for you?" Kitajima asks.

"For openers, what manner of vacsuit are you wearing?" Callahan asks with exasperation. "I've never seen anything like it."

"Something we've been working on," Kitajima said.

"I thought keeping secrets was against the law?" Zechariah said.

"Keeping secrets is, having secrets isn't," Lindsey said.

"Prove it. Tell me, what you're doing out here?" Callahan asks.

"As I've already said, we don't…"

"Yes, yes, I know, you don't disclose information prematurely to a shortimer," he glances at the damaged crate. "Whatever brought you out here is important. Otherwise, why would you reveal brand new technology, technology you have obviously gone to a lot of trouble to keep quiet." He holds his hand up stopping Kitajima from interrupting, "Don't you think I have a right to know? I live in Aldrin Station, my family lives in Aldrin Station… Now tell me, what's going on?" Little America is technically a borough within Aldrin Station but Lunarians consider it a shortimer enclave, not part of their city.

Kitajima slowly nods. "The crate contains nukes on their way to Little America from an unknown source. So maybe you can tell me, what's going on in Little America?"

"Nukes." The Inspector exclaims. "I'm sure I don't have any idea who would do such a thing."

"Excuse me Kitajima," Magi said. "Brice has finished his mapping. I've begun the simulation. This may ta…"

First Blood

Think not o' reader that those who disbelieve can ever be able to frustrate and escape Us. Their abode is Fire; what an evil resort.

Holy Qur'ân 24:57

A sudden dazzling glare that rivals the sun appears directly overhead. Tempel's visor protects his eyes and his ghost suit absorbs the sudden burst of energy like a sponge, storing it for later. The light quickly fades.

"Magi, what happened to our link with base?" Silence greets Lindsey's question. "Magi?" she repeats.

"Magi, respond," Tempel orders to no avail. Shifting his focus He asked, "Moonhawk Two. How do you read Aldrin Station?"

"All channels are unavailable and backups are not responding." The voice is sexless, common to many articulate things that do not require the sophistication of Magi. Without Magi, the default AI onboard the Moonhawk is not much more than a glorified autopilot.

"Can you determine why?" Tempel asks.

"Negative, insufficient information," the computer said.

Tempel maximizes his visor's magnification. A fading star is where Lagrange One should be and the Lunanet satellites are glitter scattered across the heavens. He links with Kitajima, "Captain, Lunanet is down. Something's happened to our satellites and Lagrange One."

"Aye, I know." Kitajima replies, having already linked with the sensors on the transports.

"Kitajima. What's happened?" Inspector Callahan demands, very bad etiquette even for a shortimer.

"A nuclear detonation somewhere near Lagrange One is affecting the entire Nearside." Kitajima replies.

"Look up. That's what's left of our communications network," Tempel said to the Inspector.

Tilting his head back, Inspector Callahan's vacsuit can't magnify enough to see the sparkle high overhead. "Are you sure? I can't see anything," he said.

"I'm sure." Tempel snaps back. His family and friends might be in danger this very instant and he's standing in the dust of Mare Nubium next to a crate of nukes talking with a clueless Federation Inspector.

"Without those satellites, we can't make contact with Aldrin Station," Kitajima said, his mind roiling over the many possibilities, not liking any. He's on his own, sitting on a shipment of thermonuclear weapons, courtesy of the Brotherhood. Who else would be shipping warheads across Luna except the Brotherhood? He must prevent delivery regardless of the price.

"I can take up a Moonhawk. Thirty kilometers straight up should make it possible to see Rim Mountain with our laser," Tempel volunteers.

"Tempel, those satellites didn't blow up on their own, they had some help. You go popping up right now, and you may attract more attention then we want. If Aldrin Station is under attack our first priority is to make sure these nukes don't fall into the wrong hands," Kitajima said.

"Under attack? Don't be absurd. Why would anyone attack Aldrin Station?" Inspector Callahan exclaims with his hands on his hips. He's a small man, well under two meters and prone to posturing. The situation is sliding out of control.

"Captain," calls Karyl.

"Report," Kitajima said.

"We're picking up low level quakes. The epicenter is in or near

Alphonsus Crater but we can't seem to pin down an exact location. It's as if there are dozens of quakes each with a slightly different point of origin. I've never seen anything like it before," Karyl said.

"We have more trouble." Tatiana said. "I see two rovers coming our way. ETA… ten minutes."

"Rovers? Are you sure?" Inspector Callahan asks incredulously. "What would rovers be doing way out here?"

"Looking for something they lost is my guess, but I'm not going to wait around to ask," Kitajima said. "Callahan, tell me straight, do you have anyone out here?"

"Absolutely not. They're not Federation," the inspector assures them shaking his head vigorously.

"Quan Kiai, link with me… Hack, get us started... stay and fight or run?" Kitajima asks.

"Run like hell," she replies.

"Aye," Quan Kiai said.

Kitajima turns to Tatiana's image, "Take, leave, or destroy the nukes?"

"Take them," she replies without hesitation.

"Aye." It was unanimous. The routine is familiar to Quan Kiai. After years of training, they almost know what the others are thinking. They all reach the same conclusion. The nukes can't fall into the hands of the Brotherhood no matter what.

Kitajima nods, "We're in agreement. Tempel, what do you need to load the crates?"

"I'll need cargo straps and three bodies. We can manhandle them into the ship," Tempel said.

"Good. Do it. Karyl, bring Moonhawk Two down right between the two crates. Consuela, set down right there." Kitajima marks their new LZ.

"Aye," they reply in unison.

"Break camp, Hack. I want to be ready to move in five minutes. Pack all the evidence and leave the instruments."

"Aye," Hack replies and starts moving.

"Inspector, I suggest you get the hell out of here. My guess is that the rovers are from Al Fahad. The timing is 'bout right and I don't think they're coming all the way out here for a picnic." Kitajima said.

"The Brotherhood would never dare harm a Federation citizen. That would be a direct violation of the Saudi Accord," Inspector Callahan replies. Even so, he sends Luke Fillmore back to the ship with orders to get it ready for liftoff.

"It's your funeral," Tempel said, shaking his head in disbelief. How many citizens have died since the UN brokered the Saudi Accord almost a half century ago? Some people never get it. Any theocracy will tell you what you want to hear, and then do whatever's necessary to grow their power. The old adage, *it takes money to make money* is magnified many times when you apply it to power. *It takes power to grab more power*. "Lindsey, have you determined how these are booby trapped?"

"Yes. It's a simple switching device just under the top," Lindsey replies. "I will disarm it later. It will remain stable as long as you don't try opening the crate." She's hastily packing up the instruments that had collected, and now contain, the raw data.

"Karyl, link to me," Tempel instructs her.

"Aye," she said.

Hack and Doc Grady are already stowing the black body bags into Moonhawk One and Tatiana's perimeter guards are returning. The area is a beehive of activity, all of it aimed at leaving in a hurry.

Karyl glides the Moonhawk across Nell's Valley, a silent leviathan a few meters above the surface. She skillfully maneuvers the craft into position.

"Snuggle your aft end up close," Tempel said.

"What girl could refuse such a tempting invitation?" Karyl purrs.

"Say when Tempel." Karyl calls out needlessly. Their linked visors provide her with an extremely accurate view of her surroundings. She knows exactly where she's going.

"When," Tempel said keeping his eyes on the ship as it settles to the ground.

The rear cargo ramp descends before the dust has settled. Tempel leaps into the back and emerges with cargo straps. Throwing a pair to Alonzo and Brice, he keeps the other two and motions for Sam and Lazarus to follow him. Handing the straps to Sam, Tempel bends down and grasps one end heaving upward, radically tilting the crate. Sam pitches the end of first one then the other strap underneath where Lazarus scrambles to retrieve them.

Without a word, Corazon and Marcel arrive on scene and assume the front positions while Sam and Tempel take the rear. Lazarus gets out of the way. One of the first things Lunarian police officers learn is how to work as a team.

"On my mark... 3, 2, 1, Up." The four Lunarians easily lift the crate, walk the short distance to the transport, depositing the load in the ships aft section. Moments later the second and third crates are sitting beside the first.

Brice and Alonzo continue securing the crates as Lindsey stows some of her instruments and goes back for more.

"We've got company." Kipper exclaims.

"Everyone onboard, *now*," Kitajima orders. "Zoey, Sam and Alonzo, stay with Moonhawk Two."

"Move it Quan Kiai." Hack calls standing at the foot of the cargo ramp.

"But I haven't finished," Lindsey said.

"Leave it." Hack replies harshly, "Unless you intend to stay."

Two vehicles leap from the ridge in a long arc, landing almost thirty meters downhill. The two humans sit in an open cockpit surrounded by a roll cage. Mounted on the top of the cage is an AK laser cannon. They kick up rooster tails of regolith as they come barreling down the slope.

Both rovers open fire. The Federation ship is the closest to them and takes the brunt of the assault. The beams slice through the thin skin. An instant later, an explosion rocks the ship. A lone figure emerges and staggers toward Moonhawk Two.

"Lieutenant, get that Moonhawk off the ground," Kitajima orders.

"Aye." Tempel reaches for the control to shut the cargo ramp. Even as the ramp starts to move, Tempel sees the Fed running towards him. He triggers the ramp to reopen and steps down where he can be seen, motioning for him to hurry. The man franticly bounds across the surface. Beyond him, the rovers race down the side of the valley firing at Moonhawk One overhead. The Fed makes it to the door and catapults himself into the transport.

Tempel triggers the cargo bay door to close. The Fed is lying beside crates. Tempel grabs him by his hard point, right between his shoulder blades, and lifts him bodily.

The survivor was the young Propriety Officer. Tempel hustles him forward, dumping him into the nearest seat.

"Help him," Tempel orders Brice.

Tempel throws himself into the pilot's seat.

"What the hell was that about?" Karyl asks harshly.

Ignoring her he said, "Keep low and move along the valley. Put the ridge between us and them," Tempel engages his harness as Karyl jerks the Moonhawk skyward and accelerates down the valley, never getting more than fifty meters off the surface.

Moonhawk One circles a hundred meters above, a tempting target for the incoming rovers. They open fire. Even at breakneck speed, the gunners will eventually hit something as big as a Moonhawk at this range.

The first significant damage is to the left forward outrigger weakening it considerably and forcing its thruster to shut down. The onboard AI compensates by adjusting the thrust vectors of the other three engines. This reduces the agility of the craft, forcing it to fly in a straight line, more or less.

Now it's an easy target. The fatal shot came in at an angle, cutting through the thin skin of the Moonhawk and striking Officer Lei Cheung in the chest. The powerful beam burns diagonally from her lower left side, plowing through her heart and lungs before emerging from her right shoulder. She never knew what hit her. One instant she was alive and breathing, the next she was not. Hot gases spew from her wound in a thick red fog trapped inside the transport. Lei is dead.

Her comrades install patches on her vacsuit trying to minimize the outgassing. If they didn't do this, vacuum would suck all the biofluids from her body and deposit it on every free surface inside the Moonhawk. This is very unpleasant.

Kitajima returns fire with the roof mounted Gatling. One of his shots punches through the front suspension of the lead rover. It buries its front axle into the lunar soil and cartwheels down the slope. One of the occupants was not strapped in. He lands hard on a basalt outcropping and doesn't move.

The second rover continues to come on hard, firing time after time, intent on making Swiss cheese out of the Moonhawk. Consuela feels her craft lurch beneath her and lose power as the right rear outrigger takes several hits. The ship is losing its ability to fly. Its onboard AI struggles mightily to make the adjustments just to keep them in the sky. As it surrenders to gravity and starts to fall, the AI tries heroically to get the remaining undamaged thrusters to compensate even more, balancing the forces on two thrusters. It doesn't have the computing power to keep them flying.

Kitajima switches the cannon to manual and keeps firing at the remaining rover to little effect. It darts behind a rock outcropping. From this protected position, it opens fire on the crippled ship.

Everyone aboard the Moonhawk has that sinking feeling one gets just before something bad happens. It's just a matter of time before that damned cannon finds its mark and blasts them from the sky.

"Prepare to abandon ship," Kitajima orders. He's firing on manual as the AI struggles to keep them airborne. They're in major trouble. The onboard AI is not good enough to engage the elusive enemy and keep the crippled ship flying. Kitajima misses repeatedly, churning up the lunar landscape around the rover while it continues to punch more holes in his Moonhawk.

Consuela and Kipper look desperately for a place to set the wounded bird down.

In the chaos inside the ship, Officer Karl Svensson loosens his upper harness and leans across the aisle to help Brice with Lei. A beam sears through the floor striking him in the chest. The beam penetrates both lungs and obliterates his aorta. He slumps in his seat, his lap belt the only thing holding him in. Karl is dead.

Risking her life, Hack unbuckles and goes to him. Wedging herself among the seats, she patches the holes, stopping the flow of blood into the cabin. More holes appear in the skin of the transport at her feet, some missing her by only millimeters. She clutches the seats for support as the craft lurches through the sky.

At that moment, Moonhawk Two sweeps over the ridge behind the rover and descends upon it. Before the Brotherhood soldiers know he's there, Tempel opens up with his Gatling on full auto. The cannon fires as quickly as the power pack can recharge it, about twice a second.

In the onslaught, he hits the rover's fuel tanks releasing clouds of hypergolic chemicals into the lunar vacuum. Another shot hit the passenger in the neck just below his helmet, slicing through the composite armor plate like a hot knife through butter, decapitating the man inside. His blood boils in the vacuum forming a red halo around the rover. The rover's hypergolic fuels mix and ignite in a silent fireball. The energy of the explosion shoves the rover into the ground, reflects off the surface, and flips the vehicle like a child's broken toy.

"Aye," someone shouted. Corazon would spend the rest of his life denying it was he.

Tempel didn't stick around. Never slowing down, he keeps the ship low and easily catches up to Moonhawk One. Reestablishing the laser link with the injured ship, He asked, "Kipper, how bad is it?"

"Bad enough. We lost two outriggers. One more and we would be part of the landscape," Kipper said.

"Can you make it fly?" Tempel asks.

"Magi could, but this glorified calculator is having major problems making the adjustments," Kipper replies.

"Maybe we can borrow enough computing power to keep it flying. Tempel, link your AI to ours," Kitajima orders.

Tempel's hands flash over the VR control panel, establishing the link and routing resources to the crippled ship.

"It's working," exclaims Kipper, surprise and relief in his voice as his ship stops descending and starts moving forward, winning the battle with gravity for the moment.

"Thank you Lord." Zechariah blurts out.

"Tempel, if we keep going on this track we will come to the Straight Fault. Have you ever been out here?" Kitajima asks.

"Aye, many times. I would venture to say that we all have. It's a great day trip." Tempel brings up a map and finds what he's looking for. "Captain, there's a large lava tube along Sunset Canyon about thirty kilometers southeast of us that runs alongside Birt Crater. It's big enough to land both Moonhawks inside."

"That's what I wanted to hear. Lay out a direct course. Get us there as soon as possible but keep the speed down and altitude low. We must minimize the risk of detection," Kitajima orders.

"Aye," Tempel said.

Moonhawk One climbs out of the valley and heads southeast followed closely by Moonhawk Two. By staying low and slow they disappear into ground clutter, all but impossible to see from orbit.

"Tempel, give me a verbal on your situation," Kitajima orders. He doesn't want to risk using the link to look for himself. That single overworked channel is the only thing keeping him in the sky.

Tempel surveys the vital signs of his crew. "Everyone is fine and the cargo's safe. We picked up the Fed Propriety Officer just before launch and he's also healthy as far as I can tell."

"I wish I could say the same. We lost Karl and Lei," Kitajima said. He personally recruited these young Lunarians to Quan Kiai and watched them grow into citizens of the highest caliber. He struggles to keep his emotions under control, but everyone knows what he's feeling. They feel it too.

ЯL

Cris heads south putting Prattville at his back, staying off the main roads. This is rough but familiar territory. Just over the next rise is Hallstead, a family owned freehold carved in the rim of a small crater.

John Jackson Hallstead immigrated to Luna over thirty years ago and founded Jackson freehold. Today, it supplies food to Darpur, Purgatory, Far Point and Aldrin Station. Hallstead contains a boarding house, repair shop, and several saloons catering to independent miners in the area. It's home to upwards of three hundred citizens, depending on the day and time.

Before cresting the rise, Cris notices a haze over the horizon, lit from underneath. He slows and edges the cycle to a point overlooking Hallstead, careful not to silhouette himself against the sky.

The scene below is horrific. Bodies lay scattered amongst the ruined buildings and shredded vehicles. The dead all wear Lunarian vacsuits.

Body fluids still boil from several and hang over the settlement like a death shroud, red with the blood of citizens. The fight here had been brutal and one sided.

Parked in the main compound are four rovers and a truck convoy. This in itself is not a surprise, but what is unusual is the lack of identification on the vehicles. Usually, the mines plaster their logos on anything that moves. These vehicles are drab gray and black camouflage. But something else is wrong with them. A normal mining convoy consists of a Goliath pulling up to fifteen carriers like a locomotive and its cars. Carriers are by necessity open at the top to dump ore inside. These carriers have sealed roofs with heavy weapons and sensors mounted on top. Airlocks and other elements identify these as human transports, not ore carriers.

A number of figures move about the compound. Some are dragging bodies into one of the buildings. Others are loading the convoy with supplies and fuel. Many more come and go freely through Hallstead's main airlock, all without the usual broadband chatter. They must be using laser line-of-sight communications. Cris zooms in but cannot see their faces, hidden behind helmets that do not transmit the wearer's expression. Instead, he sees two bulging sensor arrays, one at each apex of a triangular face. He immediately recognizes Brotherhood standard issue. Cris has great respect for the multifaceted sensor arrays that form the basis of the disparaging name, bugeyes. Despite its grotesque appearance, the array provides its wearer with a full 360° multi-frequency scan. These bugeyes aren't miners or truckers, they're clad in armored vacsuits and carry disrupters. They're soldiers.

Anger grips him as he puts it all together. Kahfah Road passes about twenty kilometers south of Hallstead as the crow flies. It's the main highway leading to the Holy City of Al Fahad. Al Fahad is the Islamic Brotherhoods biggest settlement on Luna, yet, no Lunarian has ever been inside. Access is restricted to Brotherhood. No one even knows how many reside within its walls. Factoring in the massive bombardment of Aldrin Station, Cris realizes the Republic of Luna is at war and this is the enemy.

Suddenly, several figures emerge from one of Hallstead's out buildings and begin running from the compound towards the deep ravine right below Cris. The Highlander can see these are Lunarian's from their vacsuits, a man, two women and a child of about ten years. They are frightened. Behind them, the alarm goes up and the fleeing group comes under fire from the energy weapons mounted on the massive truck convoy.

Just when Cris thinks they will all make it, the man's hit. Nothing anyone can do for him, the beam sears a hole through his chest, boiling his insides, killing instantly. The dead body limply comes to rest amidst the dust. The others disappear into the ravine with only a backward glance to their fallen comrade.

From his vantage point, Cris watches two rovers load up and start in hot pursuit. They will easily catch the Lunarians. He drops over the edge and guns his cycle down the hill, taking chances he normally would not take as he closes the gap.

This exposes Cris to fire from the convoy but none materializes. By the time he reaches the ravine, his cycle is coiled and ready to fly. Timing it to perfection, Cris launches the bike and soars over the top of the oncoming rovers, firing his pistol down at the soldiers inside.

Cris takes the lead rover completely by surprise. He shoots the driver once, his beam searing a pencil size hole through the man's armor and into his heart. The safety harness holds the body upright. A blood red fog spews from the wound. The vehicle careens off course and crashes into the side of the ravine.

The second rover swerves sideways not caring about the fleeing Lunarians. It fires its cannon wildly several times, missing badly as the cycle disappears down the ravine in the opposite direction. Slewing the rover about, they give chase, reporting to their commander as they go.

Not yet ready to quit the fight, Cris aims the cycle uphill and twists the throttle. The bike said and easily climbs up and over a bony outcrop, putting him briefly in the sights of the convoy. Several high-energy lasers churn the nearby lunar landscape, but none hit their mark. Cris disappears once more below the edge of the ravine.

Unbeknownst to either, the cycle and rover are closing rapidly on one another. Coming around a bend, Cris is the first to react and fires, taking out the driver. With a dead man driving, the rover careens sideways, hits a rock, flips, and skids to a stop on its roof.

Cris twists in the saddle and targets the exposed underbelly, shredding the fuel cell storage tanks as he goes by. The exposed toxic fluids boil into the lunar vacuum. A moment later, the hypergolic fuels mix and feed on each other, silently exploding in a monstrous fireball. Easily seen from Hallstead, the brief bright flame rising above the ravine said far more plainly than any verbal declaration, the fight has only just begun.

He guns his cycle about spewing regolith far behind him and heads east, deeper into the Highlands, making sure to leave a clearly defined track. If nothing else, he can draw the Brotherhood away from the Hallstead survivors and give them a chance. The remaining two rovers pick up his trail.

𝕬𝕷

Zechariah can't stop thinking about Inspector Callahan, the look of disbelief just before his life slipped away. This is the first time he's seen death up close and personal. Zechariah had thought coming to Luna was a once in a lifetime opportunity, one he could not pass up. Now he's not so sure. He prays for God to give him strength and to have mercy on the souls of the Inspector and Mr. Fillmore. Not once did he question why they had needed to die in the first place, simply accepting all that life throws at him as God's will. He even said a prayer for the men who had attacked them so brutally.

Lazarus and Lindsey do what they can for the young man, assuring him that he's fine and listening to him pray for strength. The effect that prayer has on him amazes Lindsey. Zechariah asks God to take away his fears and instantly calms down. Transference is a phenomenon in psychology first described by Sigmund Freud but she's never seen it operate so completely. God makes the perfect dumping ground.

For the last thirty minutes, Tempel has watched the Straight Fault, or Rupes Recta, grow ever more pronounced on the horizon. What remains of the setting sun is behind his left shoulder putting the long ridge in full sunlight, a condition that would have been brutal on unprotected eyes.

The fault extends from one horizon to the other just a few degrees off due north, running over a hundred kilometers in a straight line across the eastern Sea of Clouds. Along most of that length, the fault maintains a uniform height of almost 200 meters with a slope extending outward over two kilometers. Lunarian geologists believe the Crater Korolev impact event on the opposite side of Luna created the fault. At the time of the impact, the Sea of Clouds was a vast expanse of warm lava and would have been susceptible to a massive upheaval from a convergence of shock waves traversing the globe.

Directly in front of them, the rim of Crater Birt rises two kilometers into the lunar sky. A belt of badlands flanks the mountain extending out as far as twenty kilometers in places. Almost lost in the jumble is Sunset Canyon, a large rill that wraps itself around the base of Birt before winding out onto the Sea of Clouds. On the crater side of Sunset Canyon is a sheer basalt cliff over four hundred meters in height. Lunarians call this awe-inspiring work of nature the Wall.

Everybody has a magnificent view of the Wall during the approach. Both Moonhawks are flying less than fifty meters above the rugged desolation and creeping along at a few tens of kilometers per hour. The great expanse of stone towers over them pressing down with an almost physical force.

The terrain below continues to get rougher the closer they come. The lunar surface was shattered and broken during the craters creation event but later volcanism added to the mess. Heaving in the cooling bed of lava created a twisted tortured landscape of sharp edges and treacherous fissures. Other rills, large and small, extend outward from Sunset Canyon in a vast network. They cannot see an area anywhere large enough for even one Moonhawk to land safely, let alone two.

Less than a kilometer from the base of the cliff, they come upon a large circular depression. It's a natural amphitheater created when a section of the surface collapsed. It's over a hundred meters wide and drops vertically nearly fifty. Lava had partially filled it creating a relatively smooth plain at the bottom broken by numerous small craters. The wall of the sinkhole had given way in several places. The two Moonhawks descend into its depth.

Quan Kiai grants Lazarus privacy. From his perspective, he's alone in this place, his companions and the two ships filtered out of his vision. The constant exposure to flight has strengthened his hold over his phobia. He shudders as they drop into the hole but stays under control. The cliff face sweeps around him in a great arc. Above looms the Wall, below is the floor of the sinkhole.

Tempel takes the lead, swinging his ship north and heading across the pit. Consuela follows. Without sensors, he would have been in near total darkness, with them he can see every feature like it's a bright summer afternoon but without the glare. He likes to tweak his visual with a good dash of color enhancement to bring out the composition and structure in the rocks. Otherwise, he considers them boring. With it, the walls of the sinkhole appear a dark red, while the frozen lava lake in the bottom is a cool blue and the craters across its surface outlined in darker blue.

Even knowing it's there, the mouth of the giant lava tube is hard to see, situated right at the base of the cliff and hidden behind the rim wall of a smaller secondary crater. It's more than half filled with ancient lava. Tempel brings the ship to a hover outside leaving plenty of room for Consuela to go by.

"Consuela, do you think you can make it?" Tempel asks.

"It's going to be close. Are you sure a Moonhawk will fit?" Consuela asks.

Before he could stop himself, Tempel said "Magi…."

"Tempel you hang back and watch the clearance. If we don't fit then call out," Kitajima picks up the slack for his Lieutenant.

"Aye," Tempel said.

Tempel maneuvers in behind the other Moonhawk as it eases forward.

"Plenty of room along the sides and at least 30 centimeters above," Tempel estimates the clearance.

"Is that all?" Consuela asks nervously.

"What more do you need?" Tempel asks, knowing that Consuela will rise to the challenge.

"Caution is the hallmark of the wise. Even you should know that," Consuela said.

She adjusts the ships proximity sensors to their finest settings and creeps forward. She cannot shake the feeling of returning to the womb, only it's not her mother's warm body surrounding them, but the cold basalt of Luna. The wall is so close she has the impulse to reach out and touch it. The tunnel stretches out before her as far as she can see, lit by ship lights for the first time in its long history. The floor is smooth and flat, the arc of the walls and ceiling featureless. Consuela can almost fool herself into thinking it's man-made.

About a hundred meters in, she slows to a stop and hovers. "What do you think Kitajima? Are we in far enough?"

"Aye, far enough. Set her down as far to the right as you can."

"That's not much," Consuela said as she brings the craft down to the ground, crabbing sideways a few meters. As the thrusters shut down, she sighs heavily and relaxes for the first time since this wild ride started.

"Before we follow you in, I suggest we place a few remotes. We need some eyes and ears out here," Tempel said.

"I concur. Place a sensor at the top of the Wall and another down in the pit. Set them up for line-of-sight laser communication," Kitajima said.

"You don't think they could follow us here, do you?" Zechariah asks.

Tempel looks over at Karyl who shakes her head. Without waiting for Kitajima's response Tempel swings the Moonhawk around breaking the laser communications link and cutting them off from the other ship. Zechariah remains quiet.

Because the damaged transport is on the ground, they have access to all their AI's computing power once more. Even so, the Moonhawk rises slowly out of the sinkhole in an upward arc that terminates at the distant crest of the Wall.

"Why are we flying so slowly?" Lazarus asks.

Tempel keeps his focus on the cliff looming in front of them, "By going slow and close to the ground we are virtually invisible to anything in orbit, completely lost in ground clutter."

The instant he began talking Karyl looks sharply at Tempel. The pilot is exempt from all other duties while flying and that includes idle small talk. She has no doubt he can handle it but it makes her uncomfortable to deviate even a little from training. *By the book* is more than just a quaint saying to her.

"Ask your questions later," Karyl said. "You can talk among yourselves all you want but not with the pilot."

The top of the Wall comes abruptly. One moment they're flying up the cliff face a few tens of meters away, the next it's gone. The remainder of Crater Birt's rim mountain looms over them. Fissures radiate from the edge of the cliff. Smaller cracks are mere depressions in the regolith. Very few boulders and only sparse outcroppings break the smooth slope of the mountain rising above them.

From this vantage point, the Sea of Clouds stretches over the horizon. It's not flat like a snooker table but wavy like an ocean frozen in time. The last of the sun casts long shadows, mottling the mare's barren surface with shades of gray and black.

Tempel brings the ship down, landing well beyond the edge in perhaps the only relative flat spot anywhere atop this lunar mountain. Many other ships have landed here. He simply adds his to the mix. Human footprints are everywhere. There's nothing to erode them in this airless environment except the impacts of micrometeorites, a process taking hundreds, if not thousands, of years to see even the smallest change.

Brice and Alonzo know the drill having performed this duty many times before. They have the rear hatch wide open, the gear checked and ready to go. Brice leaps out before the transport comes to rest and heads towards the cliff edge.

Alonzo stays in the doorway watching the line play out of the wench, ready to haul Brice back at a moment's notice. The Wall has claimed its share of unwary tourists, both native and shortimer. Its edge is fragile and prone to breaking, although this area has been stomped over so many times that any loose rock has long since fallen away. But Lunarians learn early that a person doesn't live long by taking unnecessary risks.

Slowing as he approaches the cliff, Brice glances out at the view. Less than fifteen kilometers southwest, he can see the Straight Fault, the setting sun highlighting its great length.

He moves parallel to the edge, about ten meters back, looking for a fissure the right size. Spotting one, he gets down on his belly and worms forward until his head is just looking over the edge. He slips the sensor down into the crack positioning it before triggering the bladder. A small pneumatic skin fills with gas and expands, wedging itself firmly in the rock.

Brice takes a second to check his placement. Satisfied, he carefully pushes away from the edge before standing and hustling back to the transport.

Alonzo keeps Brice's tether taut as he returns. They are in and out in less than two minutes.

"Go," Karyl said as Brice slides into his seat.

Tempel lifts off, never gaining more than ten meters of altitude.

Lazarus gasps as they clear the edge, going from ten meters to many hundreds in the blink of an eye. Tempel adds to the ride by briefly putting them in freefall. Lazarus involuntarily groans and squeezes his eyes tightly shut. Less than a hundred meters above the rocky badlands Tempel guns the thrusters and stops their downward plummet in a graceful arc, sending the ship swooping across the jagged terrain. To Lazarus, they are doing hundreds of kilometers per hour, when in reality it's much less.

Tempel banks once when he's well inside the sinkhole and makes a slow graceful turn. He already has a spot in mind for the second sensor and marks it, a rocky landslide almost directly opposite of the tunnel entrance and in line-of-sight of the device they had just placed.

"Let's put this one about halfway down the slide… I'll hover at twenty meters. Alonzo, Brice, use the winch to place it. Do not leave any tracks," Tempel commands.

"Aye, no tracks." Brice said.

Alonzo has Brice in the harness by the time they reach the spot. Sliding the door open Alonzo steadies Brice as he steps out into space. He swings head down in an instant, his body at an angle to make it easier to see below him. The winch lowers him like a spider on its web.

"Move twelve meters on heading two-seventy," Brice instructs

Tempel.

Tempel complies without causing Brice to swing, a tribute to a steady hand.

"Beautiful." Brice murmurs. Moments later, he's installed the sensor and tested its alignment. Brice admires his work as he's winched up to the transport. The camouflage makes the sensor virtually invisible long before he reaches the door.

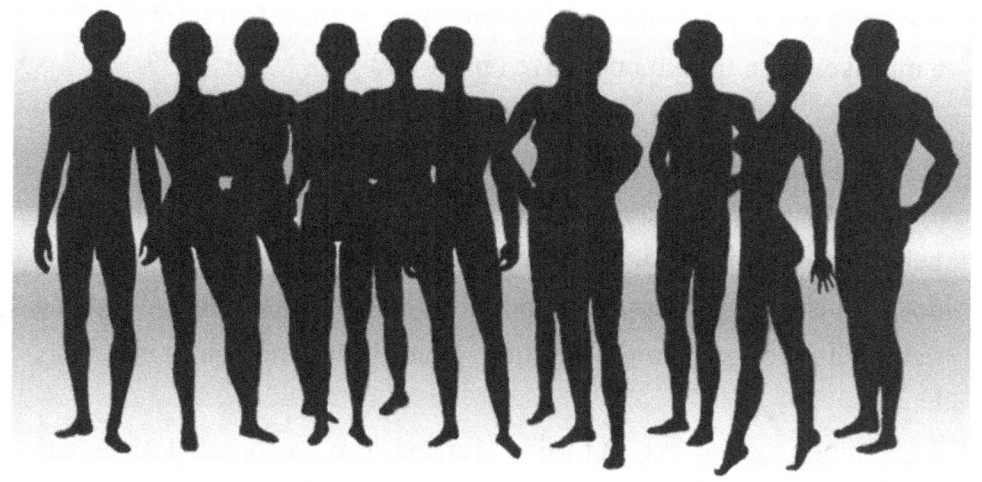

Sunset Canyon

Whosoever doeth any work in the Sabbath day, he shall surely be put to death.

Holy Bible - Exodus 31:15

Tempel eases the Moonhawk into the lava tube. He follows the fresh grooves cut into the floor and sets down close to the other ship. Kitajima, Hack and the rest of Quan Kiai are waiting. Doc Grady stands apart, dejection etched upon his face.

A stoic Kitajima waits for them to disembark, "We have two comrades to mourn but that must wait."

"There wasn't anything I could do to help them," Doc Grady said defensively.

Kitajima turns to the medico. "That's right, you couldn't save them. Now it's time to move on."

"It was my decision to wait for the shortimer. If I hadn't, Moonhawk One would have gotten clear and nobody would have been killed," Tempel said.

"Bullshit." Kitajima said forcefully. "Haven't I taught you anything?

A warrior never plays the what-if game. You can never win. If you make a mistake, learn from it and move on. Got it?"

"Aye," but Tempel remains unconvinced. He looks into Tatiana's eyes and finds hatred for the first time.

Tatiana scowls and breaks eye contact. Karl is dead. She can't believe it. Karl is dead. She doesn't blame Tempel anymore than she does Consuela and Kipper for piloting the ship or Corso for sending them out here, but Tempel's right in front of her and Karl's in a body bag.

Tempel goes to her and said, "Tatiana, I'm so sorry." Tatiana can sense his emotions almost as well as her own. He's barely holding himself together. Her arms go around his neck and she sobs into his shoulder. Tempel holds her.

Kitajima walks over to the newcomer. The young man's staring at the two warriors, "What did you say your name was?"

The question startles him but he answers, "Zechariah Hargrove." Trapped among the mutants, he silently prays for strength to see him through. His eyes betray fear.

"Inspector Callahan was a good man. I'm sorry for your loss... You're a PO?"

The man nods, "Propriety Officer First Class." PO's can popup anywhere, watching the watchers. It's normal for a PO to be young and idealistic. Their job is to ensure the Inspectors obey all religious tenets while performing their duty to the Federation.

"That means nothing out here. You do what I tell you and things will be fine. But make no mistake Mr. Hargrove, my first responsibility is to these warriors and the Republic, not to you or the Federation." Kitajima speaks the facts as he sees them without rancor or ill will.

"I understand," Zechariah replies. He's not used to people being so blatantly honest with him. It must be a trick.

"Give me your sidearm." Zechariah obeys. Kitajima flips the gun to

Hack and looks over the young man's vacsuit. It's Federation and new but uses old technology. It's devoid of power assist or electromagnet shielding, made of inferior materials, and prone to breakdowns. A few days in it would seem like an eternity.

"Brice, see what you can do to make Mr. Hargrove comfortable when you have time. This suit will need help," Kitajima said.

"Aye," Brice acknowledges.

"Here are the rules. Number one, we maintain full access to your vacsuit at all times. Number two, these warriors have the exact same authority over you that I do. You will obey their commands to the letter and without question. Number three, you will not do anything to adversely affect this mission. Number four, you will answer every question put to you fully and truthfully to the best of your ability… Disobey these orders at your own peril. I have nothing against you personally. This is just how it is. Okay?"

"Perhaps I can be of assistance," Lazarus offers.

"Now there's an idea, you baby-sit him and Lindsey can baby-sit you. That will keep everyone busy." Turning, Kitajima moves on, "Marcel and Angel analyzed the damage on our way here and they think it can be repaired. All those hits managed to miss nearly everything."

"God was looking out for us," Zechariah blurts.

"If that was looking out for us then tell him to mind his own business," Brice said glaring at Zechariah.

"I figure we have a couple hours before we can expect company." Kitajima said.

"Why would they follow us here?" Zechariah asks.

"The Brotherhood knows we have their nukes and it's a safe bet they will want them back." Kitajima said.

"Then you must destroy them. Your initial knee-jerk response to take them was in error. Destruction is the only answer. That would take the wind out of the sails of any pursuers." Zechariah's accomplished at running his mouth without knowing what he's talking about, a skill that served him well in his meteoric rise through the ranks.

Kitajima's expression deepens into a scowl when Zechariah referred to his decision as knee-jerk. "Those nukes are the only leverage we have right now. We need to figure out how to use them most effectively."

"You can't be serious. Who do you want to nuke?" Zechariah asks.

This day has gone from bad to worse and Kitajima isn't in the mood to explain himself to this Federation pipsqueak. "I haven't made up my mind. But you can be sure I will let you know when I do." he turns away from Zechariah, obviously dismissing him, trying to keep his mind focused on what needs doing to keep them breathing.

Lazarus moves up beside Zechariah and lays a hand on the young man's arm, shaking his head.

Zechariah scowls and pulls away, glaring at Lazarus. He did not appreciate the interference. "Fine, no more questions," he turns and leaves, heading back to Moonhawk Two.

"Hack, check on supplies. We need to know what we have left," Kitajima said.

"Doc, you're with me," Hack said moving purposefully towards the crippled Moonhawk. Doc Grady needs something to do and inventory is the perfect solution.

"Brice, take Marcel, Angel, Corazon and Alonzo. We need those repairs done in one hour," Kitajima said.

"Consuela, you're assigned cover-up. Make sure you fill the grooves in the floor," Kitajima orders. It's her job to erase all indications of their presence on the surface, especially outside on the floor of the sinkhole close to the tunnel entrance.

"Sam, see what you can do about reestablishing a secure link with Magi. We must find out what's going on," Kitajima orders.

"Aye," Sam nods and said, "I've already tried picking up Earthnet. All I get is static."

"Have you tried raising a ground station?" Lazarus asks her. "I mean one of the Earth based ground stations."

"Of course, but like I said, every band is swamped with static."

Lazarus raises his eyebrows, "Every band? The only thing I know of that can do that is a nuclear EMP."

"I don't think so. The effect you are thinking of needs an atmosphere to make it work. This is jamming by multiple sources," Sam said. "If I had better triangulation I think I could pinpoint their locations."

"Lazarus, go with Sam. Maybe the two of you can provide us with some answers instead of bedtime stories." Kitajima pauses and Sam heads for the Moonhawk. When Lazarus does not move, he growls, "You waiting for a written invitation? Get going. And don't forget, you're keeping an eye on the Fed."

Addressing the two copilots still in their respective ships Kitajima said, "Kipper, Karyl, stay where you are. I want you to monitor the sensors. Don't rely on the autos."

"Aye," they respond in unison.

Kitajima looks at Lindsey. "I want you to find a way to defeat active camouflage."

"How am I to do that?" Lindsey asks, "We don't have Magi and we left most of our equipment back at the crash site."

"Use your brain." Kitajima said sharply. Even during the best of times, he has very little tolerance with anybody that comes up with excuses before they even try, and the current situation leaves him even more short-tempered. He can't help but blame himself when he loses people under his command.

"My brain cannot take the place of Magi or the equipment." Lindsey retorts.

"You can use a ships AI while we're on the ground," Tempel offers.

"If any AI could do it, we wouldn't have Magi, would we?" Lindsey said.

"Just do the job you were sent to do," Tatiana said tersely.

Turning to confront Tatiana, Lindsey said, "We don't have the micro-measurement vid equipment. Do you want me to guess?" Lindsey asks.

"Just do what you can Captain Marquest, that's all I'm asking," Kitajima said, deliberately using her rank.

Lindsey gets the message and stops arguing. "Fine Captain Osaka. I will try, but no promises."

"I'm not asking for promises Lindsey," Kitajima said, turning to Tatiana, "How far did Lei get with Evolution's Child's AI?"

For a moment, Tatiana continues glaring at Lindsey as if she were an unruly child. Facing Kitajima she said, "Not very far, I'm afraid. One of them is blank and the other badly damaged. I'll need to remove the Zettasphere and reinstall it in a new interface before I will know how much data survived."

"See what you can do. I doubt if it will help us but we shouldn't ignore it," Kitajima said. Looking at the faces gathered around him, he said briskly, "The rest of you check the equipment for any damage… Let's get to it people. Show me some results."

ЯL

Inside the Moonhawk, Tatiana points and said, "If you're going to stay, sit in that seat and keep your mouth shut."

Zechariah bristles, "I'm a Federation official. You can NOT talk to me like…"

As the last syllable comes out of Zechariah's mouth, Tatiana crosses the few meters between them with supernatural swiftness, grabs him with both hands, and slams his head and shoulders into the low ceiling.

Zechariah gives a startled yelp. He panics as he struggles ineffectually against her overpowering physical strength.

Reaching the top of the ramp, Tempel leaps forward and grabs Tatiana's arm, "What are you doing? At ease lieutenant. Back off...

NOW."

With a disgusted look, Tatiana releases Zechariah and steps back. The man falls to the floor.

The entire incident lasts only moments. Zechariah grapples with what he'd just witnessed. *Lunarians are truly the spawn of Satan.*

"Have you gone mad?" Tempel asks, inserting himself between them and pushing Tatiana away from the confrontation.

"I told him to do something and he argued with me," Tatiana replies.

Lindsey helps Zechariah, putting an arm around the frightened man to steady him.

"That does not give you the right to attack him," Lindsey said.

Zechariah stares at Tatiana. Fear and isolation rip at his guts. He's on the verge of tears.

"Take it easy, Zechariah," Lindsey said, guiding him to the seat Tatiana wanted him to sit in to begin with.

Zechariah sits down and looks back up at Lindsey, "How can she move like that?"

"Drop it." Lindsey said.

"But…" he starts.

"I said drop it." Lindsey repeats, locking eyes with him. "Look, the death of our comrades is hitting everyone hard. Let's put this aside. We have enough to worry about without fighting amongst ourselves," Lindsey said turning away.

Tempel grunts and nods in agreement, "She's right. We need to work together as a team," he said pointedly to Tatiana.

"Fine," Tatiana said. "He better not argue the next time I tell him to do something."

"He won't," Lindsey looks at Zechariah who lowers his head and nods.

Turning to the damaged crate, Tempel suggests, "Let's start by going over what we do know about this shield. Lindsey, you start."

Lindsey sighs, glancing at Tatiana. "Very well." She walks over beside Tempel, "The outside is standard vacglass, common throughout the Republic." Rubbing her thumb across the inside surface where it's exposed by the damage, sensors in her gloves provide a heightened sense of feel and the identity of the materials they come into contact with. "Inside the shell is a layer of energy absorbent material similar to what I developed years ago. Sandwiched in between is some kind of solid-state layer that returns a static signal in response to an incoming beam. I was just starting to unravel it when Magi was cut off."

"How similar?" Tempel asks.

"What?" Lindsey's lost in thought.

"How similar is the energy absorbent material to what you developed?" Tempel asks.

"Virtually identical. Why?" Lindsey said.

"That goes along with Lazarus's hypothesis that the Brotherhood will buy or steal the technology instead of developing it themselves," Tempel said.

"Then where did they get the transmitter design?" Tatiana asks. "I don't know of any research on Luna into anything similar to it."

Lindsey frowns thoughtfully, her expression slowly turning into surprise, then glee, "Several months ago, a MetCal colleague of mine told me about a new technology. I didn't think much about it at the time."

"What technology?" Tatiana asks.

"It was a new way of marking items for retail. Instead of passive barcodes, they designed packaging that would store information about the object inside and relay it back on request. What it was, where it was, when it was stocked, how much it cost, that sort of thing... It would also transmit a static picture of what's inside..." Lindsey pauses as she dredges up the old memory. "As I recall, they had gotten to the point of testing prototypes of a solid-state transmitter..." she uses the ships AI to pull up a whiteboard and begins to sketch a device. "Single function, receiver and transmitter..."

To the side of the sketch she draws a solid-state Hall Effect transistor and circles it. "They claimed the power consumption was so low that the device could use the interrogating beam as its source..." She brings up the information they had obtained on the micro-configuration of the shields transmitter layer.

Tempel and Tatiana watch as Lindsey follows her train of thought to its conclusion, the confrontation all but forgotten. Here is the reason Abby had insisted they include Lindsey on the mission.

Lindsey strips away data from the image until she reaches its smallest repeating unit. Enlarging it, she pulls apart what remains with a few rapid hand movements and circles a portion. "This is the receiver/transmitter and this out here is the Hall Effect transistor and its aperture. The rest of it must be encoding of static information being sent back through the transmitter," she said excitedly. "It's elegant in its simplicity."

"That's great, but where does that leave us?" Tempel asks.

"Don't you see?" Lindsey exclaims. "The physical size of the aperture is tuned to the wavelength of our MRI beams. If we change the MRI frequency, the power source will not function."

Tempel and Tatiana perk up, looking at the sketches and then at each other. "Can we test this?" Tempel asks.

"Yes, I believe we can, quite easily." Lindsey exclaims. "Simply recalibrate a sensor, or in this case, decalibrate it."

Lindsey retrieves a portable scanner from the locker and places it on the crate, the only flat surface available in the bay. The others watch as she links into its control system and brings the calibration portion of the maintenance routine online. She writes a small program that will oscillate the frequency of the scan around the standard. Confident in her abilities, she doesn't bother testing it before running the file.

Before their eyes, the information they are receiving from the crate goes from the image of the ball valve to black, characteristic of energy absorbent shielding and back to the ball valve, cycling back and forth as the calibration program fluctuates. It's like someone turning a light switch on and off.

"Well... I'll be damned." Tempel said softly, "Very impressive." Even Tatiana has a look of grudging respect.

Zechariah keeps his mouth shut and watches.

ЯL

Sam takes the seat directly behind Kipper and Lazarus slides into the one across the aisle. Looking over at her, he links to her visor just as she links to the two remote sensors. She sweeps the sky looking for communication emission. All she finds is static.

"I've never experienced a solar storm this big but that's what this looks like," Sam said.

"Do you know of any way to cut through or filter it out?" Lazarus asks hoping that she knows something he did not.

"No, but it should fade if it's a natural phenomenon. Do you have a recording of it back at the crash site?" She asked Kipper.

"Sure," he said pulling up the data and graphically overlays it with the current signal. The intensity of the static has remained constant.

"This isn't natural. Look at the signature. A massive solar flare would be fluctuating. This is too uniform to be natural," Sam said thoughtfully.

"The last flare of this magnitude was years ago and we had plenty of warning from our solar satellites." Kipper said over his shoulder.

Sam nods. Kitajima is not going to like these numbers but she can't change physics.

Lazarus frowns and said, "It would help if we could rig up a device to determine what direction the jamming is coming from. To pinpoint the source would require something at least partially shielded from the static, something that will let us map the intensity of the radiation in a specific direction."

Without turning his head, Kipper volunteers, "Sounds to me like what you are describing is a Faraday cage. Our battle armor is a good example. The Calconn coils create a conducting enclosure and an electromagnetic shield."

"How do you propose we use battle armor to pinpoint the source?" Sam asks.

Kipper shrugs, "How should I know. You're the genius."

Sam is silent for a moment. A look of hope passes over her face. "Yes… That might just work… We can use a pulse rifle. Modify its Harmon coil to make it act as a receiver instead of an emitter." Sam is gone before either of the men can say anything.

"Relax. When she gets something in her head, it's better to let her run with it," Kipper said knowingly.

"Ok. Can we see what's going on in orbit while we wait?" Lazarus asks.

Kipper links the two of them to the visual system in the remote sensors. Like a pair of eyes hundreds of meters apart, the resulting image has excellent depth. Zooming in on the orbiting debris, they can still see sunlight glinting on the pieces as they spin in their individual orbits. "We're looking at the coordinates for Orbsat 2112. I don't think there's any doubt that it's been destroyed."

Nodding Lazarus asks, "What about Earth orbiting satellites? What can you see from here?"

"These sensors are much too small to resolve any detail on them. But maybe we can spot Heaven's Gate…" Kipper feeds in the coordinates of the orbiting station, determining that it should be in view, just minutes away from disappearing behind Mother Earth.

A bright dot with no detail is all they can see, but at least it's there. They watch as it slides from view, twinkling as it passes behind the planet. Lazarus feels an incredible sense of loss as it winks out, far out of proportion to the actual event.

"Let's take a look at Lagrange," Kipper said.

He was expecting to see the gas cloud but instead, the hulking shape of a battlestation greeted them. The torus was unmistakable even with their sensors.

"Captain. You're going to want to see this." Kipper said.

"Pull up the record just before Magi was cutoff," Kitajima orders.

The view is replaced by the original Lagrange One Space Station. In an incredible flash of light, it's gone. In its place is an expanding cloud of hot atomized gas, yellow hot at its center.

"Definitely nuclear," Lazarus said.

"Fast forward," Kitajima said.

The expansion of the gas cloud quickened and it cooled from yellow to red to a dark blue. The arrival of the battlestation was unremarkable. It eased into L1 before the gases turned blue.

"That's not good," Kitajima said.

"That's the Houris," Lazarus said. "The ridge you see here is a rail gun that runs along the outside circumference. That's over eleven kilometers."

"That's bigger than the massdriver at Longbow." Kipper said.

"And it's circular so they can send the projectiles around again, and again, and…" Lazarus said.

"We get your point," Kipper said.

"That's why they needed so much iron. The more massive this battlestation is, the more energy they can impart to the loads," Kitajima said. He turns to Lazarus, "What do you know about this ship?"

"It's new, it's big, and it's very dangerous. From L1 it dominates the nearside. Nothing is safe from it. Even your underground cities wouldn't stand a chance. It can level a section of Rim Mountain with one blow," Lazarus said.

"Lazarus, could you please come back here?" Sam asks.

"Go," Kitajima said to Lazarus. "You can tell us more about this monster later."

"I suspected the Brotherhood was planning something big but even I didn't imagine it was this big. I think the Republic is at war. I think we're fighting for our lives," Lazarus said as he rises.

"Tell me something I don't know," Kipper said.

Lazarus moves through the passenger compartment. He finds Sam at a fold down workbench in the storage bay, the pieces of a pulse rifle scattered across it. She's taken the rifle and secured it in a tripod mount. It points almost straight up.

Motioning him to stand next to her she said, "I've reversed the voltage on the Harmon coil creating a perfectly shielded space in its interior. No electromagnetic static or electric field emissions can get in except through the muzzle. Now watch."

She slowly moves the tip of the Harmon coil back and forth in a small arc. The graph spikes sharply when the device is pointing in one very specific direction. She continues to rock it back and forth giving him a feel for the narrow angle, just a few degrees wide.

"What lies in that direction?" Lazarus asks.

"Nothing that I know of," she said, "It's simply a spot in orbital space. There's many others like this."

"Captain, we have company." Kipper broadcast.

Brice scrambles to shut down the nano-repair interface, difficult to do even under normal circumstances. Angel is lying on her stomach atop the outrigger, feeding raw material to the damaged sections. The rest of the platoon links to the remote sensor on top of the Wall. The ship is about two kilometers out and a thousand meters up flying slowly on a course parallel with the Wall, directly down Sunset Canyon.

"Let's shut it down, people," Kitajima orders.

Kipper and Karyl power down the two Moonhawks except for the AI core memory. All interpersonal communications cease, isolating everyone.

The world turns pitch black and silent. Lazarus reaches out where Sam had been only moments before, touching her.

Sam leans over cradling his head in her hands and puts her forehead against his, "Relax, this will be over in a few minutes," her voice is distant but understandable.

Without their lights, the tunnel is pitch-black. As the minutes drag, Lazarus becomes more and more convinced that something has gone terribly wrong. If it wasn't for Sam's firm grip holding him steady, he might have lost it and done something incredibly stupid.

After what seems like hours, his vacsuit powers up. Sam is there next to him.

She smiles and said, "That wasn't so bad."

Lazarus manages a weak smile, "Did I mention that I'm afraid of the dark?"

Sam chuckles, "You hide it well... Do you want to see the sensor data?"

"Yes, of course," Lazarus replies.

Sam links his visor with the data stored on the remote sensors and begins playback at normal speed.

Once again they see a ship approaching. As the craft draws near, a second ship flying much lower, darts back and forth across the badlands obviously looking for something or perhaps presenting itself as a target trying to lure them out. The lower ship swoops into the sinkhole almost directly in front of the remote sensor hidden in the landslide. This ship is very different from a Moonhawk. Where the Lunarian ship is smooth and pleasantly proportioned, this is boxy and angular, built of bolts and beams. Much smaller than a Moonhawk, it bristles with disrupter cannon. The little ship must be a flying power plant to support them all. There could be room for only one or two pilots. It was strictly an offensive war machine with very little defensive capability. It darts about the sinkhole but leaves without getting near their hiding place.

"They'll be back," Kitajima promises. "Brice, how are we doing?"

"The underlayment is done and we are closing. Should be only a few more minutes,"

"Good. Quan Kiai… Company meeting in five minutes between the transports," Kitajima orders. "Brice and Angel have the only free pass unless they're done by then. By the numbers, acknowledge."

In rapid succession his officers report in. "Lindsey, Lazarus, Zechariah. You're all invited." Kitajima said.

A few minutes later Quan Kiai begins arriving, the officers segregating themselves to one side, Zechariah, Lindsey and Lazarus the other. Kitajima is surprised to see Sam standing beside Lazarus, a worried expression on her face.

Kitajima takes center stage and looks at her expectantly, "Sam, what have you got?"

"We managed to determine that the interference blocking our communications is coming from multiple regions of orbital space. The static is steady and doesn't appear to be letting up any time soon. Until they stop jamming, we don't have a prayer of contacting Aldrin Station or in raising an Earth ground station," Sam reports.

Kitajima pauses, thinking. "So communications is being jammed across the entire system?"

"That's how it looks. No one in orbital space is communicating except by laser."

Kitajima goes on, "Tempel, what have you to report?"

"Lindsey was able to determine how the active camouflage works and a way to see past it. We have already begun modifying our sensors. The ships sensors are complete and we have only a few ghost suits remaining, Brice, Marcel, Angel, Hack and yours," Tempel reports.

"Good. Well done Lindsey. Tatiana, did you find out anything from the damaged AI?" Kitajima asks.

"The Zettaspheres external interface suffered heavy damage and without specialized equipment, which I don't have, I risk further damage," Tatiana said.

"Is there something else?" Kitajima asks recognizing the signals. She's something to say, and is dragging her heels.

"Well... After coming to this conclusion, I had some time and brought up the reconstruction Brice was doing when we bailed at the crash site. Magi had pretty much finished it and I had the ships AI run what she had done. I think you should see it," Tatiana said.

"Very well," Kitajima said.

The vid begins at the crash site just as they had found it, debris scattered along a two-mile track angled across the valley reaching the far side. The three dimensional image rotates to give the observers the best possible angle as it begins to roll backwards, like a video in reverse. Bit by bit, each piece twists and moves backward in time, retracing the path of their arrival, slowly at first but building up speed. The gouges and scars in the landscape disappear as the dust and debris return.

The crates pick up speed as they travel back in time. A huge cloud of regolith shrouds the freighter's main cabin as it tumbles and rolls across the valley floor, obscuring detail. It's not clear when the cargo came loose but Magi had made an educated guess that it was early in the crash because of the lack of more damage to the crates. The crates and the cabin continue to reverse their course towards the instant of impact, dust and debris swirls around them. Other smaller pieces of the engine compartment and the thrusters themselves cartwheel across the flat terrain, all converging towards that point in time and space when they were last together.

As the simulation approaches this point, a huge wall of dust and rock erupts from the surface blocking their view of the ship. Evolution's Child had acted like a giant snowplow after it hit but before it reached the bottom of the valley and started to tumble. This material is returning to where it had lain undisturbed for untold millennia. Tatiana halts the presentation and rotates it until they are looking almost straight down at the wreck before allowing it to continue. She stops it once more just as the crates and cabin come together. Seen through a veil of debris, the crates come to rest in the cargo section of the freighter, all four of them.

The group is silent as the implications sink in.

Kitajima looks at his officers. There's a good chance that some of them will not see home again if they do what needs doing.

"Captain, we must to go back and deal with this," Tempel said quietly, voicing what nearly everyone has already concluded.

"Yes Lieutenant, I believe you're right," Kitajima said softly.

"Are you nuts?" Zechariah said too loudly, panic in his voice. He can't understand them even considering such an idea. It's suicidal. Tatiana gives him a look that sends him ducking behind Lazarus.

Kitajima looks intently at Hack, "Get us started."

"What if we destroy the nukes we have and go after the one's we don't?" Hack asks. Quan Kiai knows the drill.

"Why not use one of the nukes we have and take out the one's we don't?" Tempel suggests looking sideways at Hack.

"You are assuming the other crate is still there. What if it's already gone?" Tatiana asks.

Tempel looks steadily at her for a moment, both of them coming to identical conclusions, "We have no choice. We must go back and find out what's going on. They may not have found the other crate or they may even think we have them all. We don't know what the situation is back at the crash site, and we need that information to make the best decision."

"It's suicide to go back. We just managed to get away. Two of your friends are dead, for God's sake." Zechariah exclaims, ignoring Lazarus's attempt to silence him.

"I didn't see God back there, only Brotherhood." Tempel replies.

Kitajima raises his hand stifling any more comments. Turning to Zechariah, "This is our responsibility, not yours," Turning back to face them he continues, "Anybody see it different? Or do you think we should pull in our tails and convince ourselves the job is done?" Kitajima looks out among the faces of his young Lunarians and can find no doubt, no hesitation in any of them. They all know what needs doing and will do it.

"Captain, we know our duty," Tempel said.

"I didn't come along to be left behind," Lindsey said with conviction. "I may not be Quan Kiai but I can still fight."

"As can I," Lazarus impulsively adds.

Kitajima stares at them, venting a few chuckles that soon evolve into a belly-busting eye-watering incredulous guffaw. His officers join in until they're all in tears, their tension shattering like an overstressed pane of glass. Lindsey and Lazarus stand and stare at the spectacle blankly. Lindsey cannot help but smile. Lazarus shrugs. Zechariah looks on, his eyes narrow with suspicion, not sure what is happening, thinking they may all be crazy.

Kitajima gets himself under control as he walks over to them. "Lindsey, Lazarus," he said slowly looking at each in turn. "I appreciate your offer…" he pauses, barely refraining from laughing point blank in their faces, "As I said, you will not be asked to fight, whatever it is we decide to do."

Turning away, Kitajima asks, "How are we on supplies Hack?"

"1200 hours of air and plenty of water and food but short on fuel. We received too many hits in the hydrazine tank. It's essentially empty. We were lucky we didn't take one in the aniline."

"BOOM." Brice said loudly, grinning when Zechariah jumps.

"Knock it off Brice," Tempel said.

Brice grins and obeys.

"Bottom line, once we divide the hydrazine in Moonhawk Two, we won't have enough to go back to the crash site and get us home. Pick one or the other," Hack reports.

"That settles it. How can you fight without fuel?" Zechariah injects.

"Leaving the Brotherhood with three nukes is not an option." Kitajima is growing tired of repeating himself.

Zechariah shakes his head and turns away in frustration. He's convinced God is talking to his heart and is dismayed that he cannot persuade these people of it.

"Let's take a step back, shall we?" Kitajima said abruptly. "Let's stick to the facts and decide what our next move should be." Turning to Hack He asked, "Where is the nearest cache?" For the last four years, Corso has had emergency supplies placed in various hidden locations out on the Central Highlands intended for just this situation. All they had to do was find one.

Hack shakes her head, "Nothing way out here. Anybody know different? Got your own personal stash out here somewhere?" She looks around at Quan Kiai.

A few shake their head but nobody said a word.

"Do we know how bad Aldrin got nailed?" Brice asks the question on everybody's mind.

Kitajima shakes his head, "Not really. The city could be under Brotherhood control right now."

"We don't have the hydrazine to make a run south to Shennong." Hack said. "The closest settlement of any size is Scottsbluff to the west of us in Faye crater. It's about seventy kilometers closer than Aldrin and by my calculations we can just make it, even after we retrieve the nukes."

"Then I guess we're going to Scottsbluff," Corazon said.

"I've been to Scottsbluff. There isn't much there," Angel points out.

"This isn't a vacation," Kitajima said. "I don't see another choice. We will head for Scottsbluff after the raid. Anybody have any other thoughts?"

"What are we going to do with Lindsey, Lazarus, and our young Propriety Officer while we fight?" Hack asks.

"Why don't we leave them somewhere? We can come back and pick them up after we're done," Brice said.

Lindsey looks at him with annoyance and back at Kitajima, "I will not be dropped off like some package. You are not the only one who came on this operation knowing what's at stake. We all knew it was a military mission. You do what you need to do and we will stay out of your way. Just stop this talk of leaving us behind."

Kitajima nods, "Good. Lindsey, you're in charge. You'll be responsible for making sure Zechariah and Lazarus do nothing. You will all be isolated. I cannot risk having any of you confusing us with your inexperience. End of discussion," he growls as Zechariah starts to speak, "That's the way it will be. You're not to even get out of your seats. You'll sit quietly and do nothing. Is that clear?" Kitajima leans down, looking meaningfully at Lindsey.

"Aye Kitajima, it's clear. Can we observe? Or must we wait until the vid's released," Lindsey said. She believes it's her duty as a citizen to be with these young Lunarians. She wants to know what price her freedom. How can she make intelligent decisions if she's unaware of their cost? How can anyone?

"It's your right to observe, but you'll only see what the officer is seeing, nothing more. You'll not be able to communicate with any officer or change their sensors remotely," Kitajima said. "The only exception is this… If you feel it necessary, call and I'll respond, but it had better be one hell of a good reason. Is that understood?"

"Aye." Lindsey nods her thanks. She has no desire to do more than watch the coming battle.

Kitajima uses his visors Map and Terrain Function (MTF) to present a 3D image of the territory around the crash site. Quan Kiai gathers around the waist high map.

The mare in that region consists of a number of wide valleys in a washboard pattern running parallel with Nell's Valley. They're giant ripples that solidified in the lake of lava billions of years ago. At this scale, the image looks like a frozen sea, only these wave crests are ridges of stone. Kitajima walks into the map. It cuts him off at the waist. He circles a position, his finger leaving a thin red line. A tiny transport appears at its center as the line fades.

"Hack, you bring Moonhawk One to this spot. I will land Two here. How many bugs do we have?" Kitajima asks her.

"Ten, all standard issue," Hack said.

"Good. Let's each send a pair into the valley as soon as we set down." Studying the map display carefully, Kitajima makes several line-of-sight comparisons, his system virtually placing him at each possible location, letting him see for himself. He decides on a high ridge overlooking the crash site from almost a kilometer away.

"While the bugs are snooping, Sam will position a spybot here," a bright white pinpoint of light appears within the terrain, "and Kipper will set another here." Another marker appears. "That will give us line-of-sight communications all across the valley. As soon as we have the data from the bugs we'll finalize our attack plan." Looking up at his young warriors he continues, "We may not need to fight but if we do, you will fight with extreme prejudice. I don't want to see any good sportsmanship when I review the logs. Understood?"

"Aye." The young police officers are tired of running and hiding, ready to avenge the deaths of Lei and Karl and all those people in Lincoln County Hospital. This is war and their enemy will receive no quarter.

"Ok people, let's break out the weapons and get mounted. It's time for the Republic to hit back." Kitajima said grimly.

"Aye," a ripple of excitement passes through the company.

"Hack, before we lift, I want you to install shape charges on the nukes. No matter what happens, we can't let the Brotherhood have them back." Kitajima said.

"Aye," she said.

Satisfied, Kitajima nods and said, "Let's get locked and loaded. You have thirty-four minutes until liftoff."

ℜ𝕃

In 480 BCE, three hundred Spartans under King Leonidas helped one another prepare for the battle of Thermopylae. So too does Quan Kiai help one another don the lethal accoutrements of 21st century warfare, Lunarian style. They have done this many times, but today's different. The usual chatter's absent.

Tempel runs Sam's diagnostic finding everything in the green. "You're good."

Waiting until Sam is ready, Tempel lifts the hard shell of his Shoulder Mounted Gun Platform (SMGP) over his head sliding it down onto his shoulders. He raises his arms straight up letting Sam activate the molyseals. The SMGP harness cinches tight under his arms and across his chest without hindering body movements. It provides a stable platform for attaching a pair of weapon mounts. Tempel is aware the moment the weapon system integrates with his ghost suit and comes online.

In the mount above Tempel's left shoulder is a disrupter. Short barreled and lethal, it uses the latest Harmon coil technology enhanced by a Lunarian innovation known as superconductive plasma discharge, something entirely new in the world of high-energy beam weapons. Mass is added by injecting a pulse of plasma, called a slug, into the energy stream. Arriving behind the beam at twenty kilometers per second, the slug strikes the target with incredible physical force. The one-two punch devastates ceramic armor, the beam weakening it, then the slug punching through.

Above his right shoulder is a launcher containing a dozen SuperX missiles. Propelled by magnetoplasma thrusters, they are capable of tremendous accelerations yet maneuverable enough to fill the role of close support. With a guidance system smart enough to stay on moving targets, they are the fire and forget weapons in the arsenal.

Look-and-shoot technology has been around for well over a century. To select a target, Tempel simply looks at it. What is unique is that Tempel picks which weapon and fires it using Direct Mind Control (DMC). Developed at the turn of the century for paraplegics, he has a neuromotor prosthesis embedded in his motor cortex, the area of his brain responsible for voluntary movement. The device detects brain cell activity and converts it into external signals. Thus, to fire his disrupter, he looks at the target and flexes his fire muscle, much in the same way he would locate a cup and close his hand around it. Tempel has trained to the point that he doesn't need to think about how to do it anymore, he functions as if this were a natural part of his being.

Sam's diagnostic is in the green. "You're good."

"Aye," Tempel links with Lazarus.

Lazarus is talking. "I think the Brotherhood is making a bid to control orbital space and the powersats. If they succeed, they'll dominate Earth and be in a position to dictate to everyone. That would make them the world's first multi planet empire."

"To control the powersats they must control Taurus Colony and Luna. That means controlling Lunarians." Lindsey said from inside where she's helping Hack rig the crates. "That's the only viable reason for these bombs. We outnumber them at least ten to one. But if they can threaten us with a nuclear bomb…well… that evens things out quite a lot."

"That's their style," Lazarus said nodding. "How many nukes do you think it would take to hold Luna hostage?" He asked. "Aldrin Station,

New London, Shennong, Kyoto, Gagarin."

"That's five but Evolution's Child carried twelve rather small nukes. How do you explain that?" Tempel asks while walking over.

Lazarus turns to face Tempel, shrugs and said, "How many boroughs are there in Aldrin Station, ten, eleven? What if each borough gets a nuke? Even if they are small, that many going off all at the same time would definitely destroy a Lunarian city," Lazarus said. "I don't believe they simply want to subdue Luna. I think their long range goal is to destroy you and take what is yours, your cities, your factories, your women…"

"Our women?" Tempel asks.

"Absolutely." Lazarus said. "The Brotherhood considers women, especially little girls, as spoils of war. Don't cut them any slack, because they won't cut you any."

"You needn't worry. Quan Kiai will make sure their willingness to die for Allah is fulfilled," Tempel replies. The image of three-year-old Lana rises unbidden within his mind, blond hair, sweet voice, and pancake syrup smeared across one cheek. The syrup turns to blood as Lana becomes just another body in the wreckage. He shakes his head to clear his mind of these dark thoughts.

"Why bring the nukes in this way? Why not bring them as part of the invasion?" Tatiana asks joining the conversation. "Shipping them in on a freighter like ordinary cargo makes no sense to me."

"Deniability perhaps? If Minister bin Aunker has one weakness it's that he's overly cautious. If Brotherhood forces are caught with them, the gig is up," Lazarus replies. "They must have gone through several checkpoints to even get them off the planet. That's got to be it. He just didn't want to risk getting caught."

Tempel checks in on the young Federation Propriety Officer. Not long ago, polygraphic indicators had shown Zechariah suffering from a high degree of tension, but that seems to have changed. The man is almost too calm as he leans forward, head bowed, eyes clinched shut, and fingers clasped together, praying to his god.

"…hold me in your hand dear Lord. Do with me as you will. In the precious name of Jesus Christ, Amen." Zechariah finishes. He raises his head slowly, his face the picture of tranquility.

Tempel shakes his head in bewilderment. Religion has brought them to this point. He's incapable of distinguishing between Islam and Christianity. They're both Iron Age superstitions motivating otherwise peaceful men and women to do things they would never consider doing without it. He glances at his comrades, proud that none of them suffers from the god delusion and the empty promises of an afterlife. Yet, they are willing to risk everything for family, friends, and freehold.

Tempel's curiosity is aroused. It's not often he's in such close contact with a devout Christian. Even though Freedom of Belief is among the rights listed in the Lunarian Constitution, there's simply a dearth of god believers among Luna's general population. It's no fun to argue with someone with the same set of values as you have and arguing is one of Tempel's favorite pastimes.

"Zechariah, you'll be riding in the other transport. Come outside and join us," Tempel orders.

Zechariah exits the Moonhawk and stops beside Lazarus.

"Where do you want me to sit?" Zechariah asks.

"Someone will tell you when its time," Tatiana replies.

Zechariah glances at Tatiana then at Lazarus. A strangeness flashes across his face.

Zechariah is hiding something. "What do you know about Lazarus?" Tempel asks.

"Nothing…" but the question rattles him.

Tempel bores in, "You're lying. I will ask you one more time. What do you know about Lazarus?"

Zechariah's polygraphic indicators are now swinging wildly, the calming influence of the prayer has evaporated and raw fear takes its place.

"He's a traitor. A memo was sent around ordering us to watch for him." Zechariah said.

"What did the memo order you to do when you found him?" Tatiana asks moving closer to him.

Sweat runs down Zechariah's face, "Report his location."

"Another lie... Captain, what's the punishment for lying?"

Zechariah panics, "The memo said to either bring him in or administer justice ourselves. They promised an early return home with full pay and honors for the one who... does him." Turning to Lazarus, "They have Saul," he blurts out.

"What." Lazarus lunges at Zechariah who backs out of reach. With one hand, Tempel easily holds Lazarus back. "My brother had nothing to do with my leaving."

"Then you must come back with me and tell them. You are the only one who can save him now. His life's in your hands."

Tatiana huffs, "Let me get this straight. The Federation puts a hit out on Lazarus, arrests brother Saul who has done nothing illegal and the only way to save him is for Lazarus to turn himself in, and if he doesn't, it will be Lazarus' fault whatever they decide to do to Saul... Now there's the Federation the world has come to love. No act too despicable, no deed too dreadful, the end justifies the means."

"They have forgotten that the path is as important as the destination," Kitajima said. "Thank you Zechariah."

The young PO turns to look for Kitajima, spotting him under the newly repaired outrigger with several others. "Thank me for what?"

"For reminding us who we are by showing us who we are not," Kitajima smiles, "Thank you."

Zechariah shakes his head in confusion, "I don't understand."

"Of course you don't. Tell me, how do you feel about Saul being punished in place of Lazarus?" Kitajima asks Zechariah.

"I… think it's wrong," Zechariah said.

Tatiana laughs again, "Liar." she steps towards the young man who moves behind Tempel.

"OK. OK. The truth. Lazarus was in a position of trust and betrayed that trust. He is an enemy of the Federation. Besides, he knew his brother would be under suspicion when he left and didn't care," Zechariah said.

"I…" The accusation hits Lazarus like a ton of bricks. Can he tell himself he was not aware of that possibility? No. He knew this could happen and closed his mind to it.

"You cannot lay this evil on him," Tempel said. "Lazarus fled a corrupt system because that was his only option. Citizens no longer have a say in what's done in their name. When a government gets that bad, only revolution can change it."

"That's terrorist talk." Zechariah hisses.

"One man's terrorist is another man's freedom fighter."

"I will not listen to such ungodliness." Zechariah said.

"If everything happens according to god's plan, why not the fall of the Federation?" Tempel asks.

"I know God's plan and destroying his kingdom on Earth is not part of it." Zechariah flares.

"How do you know? Do you hear voices?" Tatiana asks.

"When I pray, *He* places the answers on my heart."

"Maybe that's indigestion," Tatiana said.

"You don't honestly believe you have conversations with the creator of the universe… do you?" Tempel asks.

"*His* will be done. I simply lay my case before *Him*."

"If god is willing to prevent evil but is not able, then he's not omnipotent. If god is able but not willing then he's malevolent. If god is both willing and able, then where does evil come from? If god is neither willing nor able, then god is not a god at all." Tempel stares down the young man. "I lost family in Lincoln County Hospital. Where was your god then?"

Zechariah wilts under Tempel's glare, "I'm not your enemy Lieutenant, and **God** is not your enemy. As a Christian, I believe as you do, in the sanctity of life. But I also realize even the Creator finds it necessary to occasionally take life in order to save life. What the Lord gives, **He** can take away."

Tempel turns to Lazarus, "How did you live with such nonsense?"

Lazarus shrugs. "As a child, I can remember my father speaking to me of things I didn't understand at the time. As I grew older, I realized he was a Freethinker hiding behind a facade of belief in order to survive. I learned from a real pro."

"I can't imagine lying about something so big for so long. To pretend to believe in god, attend church, pray, and say all the things you must have said to convince everyone around you that you are a Christian. How did you do it?" Tempel looks at Lazarus strangely.

"It's dishonest," Brice adds. His expression verges on distrust.

Lazarus shrugs, "I kept reminding myself of something my father once told me. He said not to worry about telling a lie just as long as the person you lie to, is lying back at you. The people that fill the churches pretend to be one thing but are something completely different. I fit right in."

Zechariah frowns, thinking about this for a moment, "What about true believers? How do you justify lying to them?"

"What makes you think you're not lying just because you believe what you're saying? To me the most despicable lie is the one retold by someone foolish enough to believe it," Lazarus said. Turning to Brice, "The essence of a good lie is to put some truth in it and believe it or not, you can find truth in the bible. For instance, Ecclesiastes Chapter 3, verses 18-19. *I hoped in my heart that God might make clear to the sons of men, that they themselves are beasts. For that which befall the sons of men, befall the beasts; as the one dies so dies the other, yea, they have all one breath; so that a man hath no preeminence above a beast.*"

Tempel grins, "I'm starting to see how you managed."

"I hate to end this little chitchat but it's time to mount up," Kitajima said.

Battle of Nell's Valley

"Courage without conscience is a wild beast."

Robert Ingersoll (1833-1899)

Kitajima lands his Moonhawk northwest of Nell's Valley, a few kilometers from the crash site. Moments later, he releases a pair of bugs, small self-contained recording devices the size of a mosquito whose primary mission is to locate all electronic sentries, and second, obtain a visual on the crash site. One is to fly along the ridge closest to them and the other out over the valley. Both will remain several hundred meters up, very difficult but not impossible to detect. If detected, other bugs could follow them back. Everyone is on edge, alert to the possibility of fight or flight on very short notice.

Sam puts the final touches on the little spybot, filling it with just enough fuel to get it where it needs to be. Even a few grams left in the tanks could attract the attention of a passing sniffer. Like the bugs, it deploys using micro-thrusters to propel it through the lunar vacuum. The spybot contains a full remote sensor array and a complete set of combat communications in a package the size of a peach pit.

Sam's the acknowledged champion in deploying spybots. She's managed to put them in impossible places more than once during training. Now, when it really matters, she relies on that training and doesn't let herself think about the consequences of failure.

Sam flies the spybot as if she were sitting in a tiny cockpit within the stone. She streaks up the valley staying low, never more than a few meters off the surface. Stopping below a ridge, the spybot creeps upward until she can just peek over the top. It hovers there for an instant while she looks about.

Nothing.

Sam darts over to rest briefly on the top of a prominent boulder, and then flits away. Like bread crumbs marking a path, she leaves behind a device smaller than a grain of rice, a line-of-sight laser communications relay. She maneuvers over the ridge and starts down the other side.

Still nothing.

The spybot crosses the valley floor and up the far side. Sam glances at her fuel meter. She must pick up the pace or risk not getting the bot where it needs to be.

This section of the valley is rugged and broken. A small cliff lies before her. Up the rock face she flies, cresting it just as the fuel warning sounds in her ears. With less than thirty seconds of flight time remaining, she maneuvers between boulders at blinding speed. She slows and lands the flying piece of basalt on top of a pile of stones similar to her tiny spybot, its sensors pointing into the valley below. Shutting off the tiny thrusters, Sam looks at her remaining fuel. Only two seconds of flight time remaining. She releases a long breath, shaking her head in disbelief.

"Well done." Kitajima said squeezing her shoulder. "Establish the comm link with Hack."

Sam tentatively probes the coordinates and is gratified with an immediate acknowledgment. The two transports are linked once more.

"Hack, report," Kitajima orders.

"We're at our assigned position awaiting our bugs return," Hack said.

"Good. Let me know when you get them back," Kitajima said. "Tempel, let's take a look."

"Aye," Tempel replies.

Linking to the spybot, Tempel zooms in on the camp. From this low angle, it's impossible to see everything but there's more than just a few rovers. At least one big ship, several heavily armed Goliaths, and two of the small fighters are parked on the other side of the crash site, perhaps even the same two that was looking for them back at Sunset Canyon. Movement is everywhere and he can just see the top of a large portable shelter.

At that instant, two rovers come over a rise directly into their field of view completely blocking the camera. Tempel backs off the magnification. These are more of the small two man rovers they had tangled with just a few hours earlier. For their size, they pack a big punch, not much more than four wheels on a high capacity power pack feeding a disrupter. Quan Kiai respects the lethal cannon mounted on these vehicles. They have the power to punch through their vacsuit's shielding with a single shot.

Tempel begins to populate the strategic map of the engagement. Refocusing on the main camp, he continues to categorize the Brotherhood's forces, the number of people, type of armament, and the location of everything. This is something he's particularly good at, identifying what they are up against in a way that enables them to formulate a plan of action.

"There must be a hundred guys there," Brice whispers. "Are you sure we want to do this?"

Tempel's hands fly over his virtual controls. Without looking up or slowing down, he grins. "What? You want to live forever?"

"Hack, are you seeing this," Kitajima asks.

"Aye... It looks like we have some work to do," Hack said. "The big ship is a Brotherhood frigate. If it brings its guns to bear, we'll be in trouble."

"Excuse me, but our bugs are back," Sam reports, already putting them in the reader. She brings the first vid online.

The bug, programmed to fly parallel with the ridge, doesn't detect any electronic sentries. On the other hand, the human sentries are easily located. They're clumped up beside a rocky outcropping directly above the site. Tempel counts twelve, all with pulse rifles. They seem more interested in what's happening down in the valley than keeping an eye on the mare. On the slope below the ridge are other rovers and their soldiers clustered in groups of two or more. Tempel's hands blur as he organizes the data for the simulation.

The other bug went down the heart of the valley and directly over the crash site itself. From hundreds of meters up, its view is remarkable. Men and equipment swarm over and around the wreckage. Most are common soldiers but some technicians are apparent. As the bug passes over the pilothouse, it becomes clear what they're doing. There's a trench alongside the pilothouse and even as they watch, an excavator emerges with a load of lunar regolith, dumping it close by.

A group is standing next to the entrance of the pit talking and gesturing. Tempel wishes he could eavesdrop on the conversation.

"They haven't got them yet." Sam declares.

The bugs directly above the main camp now, a hastily constructed affair made up of a portable shelter and three Goliaths parked in a row. He had landed on the very same spot just hours before. As the bug loops back towards them, it flies over several clusters of rovers with their crews lounging in or around them. It's plain to everyone that this is not going to be a walk in the park.

The bug passes over the two fighters. These machines pose high danger to the company, perhaps greater than the frigate. It would jeopardize the entire mission if even one of these deadly little ships gets skyborne. The bug identifies another vehicle, this one sitting apart from the rest, probably the hypergolic fuel tanker.

Kipper and Tatiana incorporate the information from their bugs and combine it with the data Tempel has collated. Even though the two ships are kilometers apart, VR brings them together around an integrated 3D image of Nell's Valley, the frigate, fighters, Goliaths, and rovers all clearly represented in miniature.

Kitajima moves forward looking like a man wading in waist deep water and takes a position at one end of the valley. "I will start the ball rolling by taking out the frigate's comm system and armament. That ship is my primary target. I don't want it to ever see orbital space again... Tatiana, you will attack the fighters, don't let them get off the ground. Then drive through to the main camp from here... Tempel, your team attacks from this direction, take out that bunch on the ridge and proceed to the main camp this way... Kipper you will attack from this direction and Consuela from here. Do a pincer and close the loop... I want everyone to converge and take everything out. I don't want any men or machines left in one piece... Once the camp is clear, Hack will land here. I will bring in my ship and take this position. Brice and I will assume responsibility of extracting the crate. The rest of you will spread out and find whatever the Brotherhood has been kind enough to leave behind. Memory cubes, command and control computers, any AI's, you know the drill. Let's do this by the book. Find everything of value and destroy the rest. Any questions or comments?" He looks around at the faces of the assembled officers, looking for weakness or hesitation and finding none. "Good. Let's do a full scale simulation and see where we are."

Quan Kiai plays a sophisticated game of team combat, a virtual dose of warfare that allows them to experience the coming battle before risking their lives, correcting the flaws in the plan while giving the young warriors confidence. Fifteen minutes later, they're finished, having coordinated targets and responsibilities for the attack right down to what weapon to use in each instance. Time well spent.

"Anybody want to add anything?" Kitajima is proud of the way his team's performing.

"Aye, I do," said Tempel.

"Go ahead, speak your mind."

"I just want to remind everyone of Lincoln County Hospital, of Black Friday, of Prattville and Darpur and countless others. The men we face today applaud mass murder and support the leaders who ordered these killings. Don't feel sympathy for any of them. They deserve no mercy."

The gathering listens solemnly. Too many family and friends died at the hands of the Brotherhood. They all feel the weight of those innocent Lunarians and honored to be the tool of their vengeance. They hoped this moment would come when they put on a ghost suit. Quan Kiai is ready for the coming battle, a weapon of mass destruction primed for detonation.

"Are we set?" Kitajima asks one last time.

"**Aye. Locked and Loaded**," the young warriors reply.

Kitajima leans forward and thrusts his right fist into the sky, "Quan Kiai."

The others join him and their fists come together in a tight circle and say in unison, "**Quan Kiai.**"

"Let's roll," Kitajima utters the words that send Lunarian warriors into battle for the very first time.

ЯL

Lazarus takes the seat behind Kitajima and next to Lindsey. Zechariah sits by himself at the back.

"How long do you think they'll be?" Lazarus asks.

Lindsey is tense, "As long as it takes. We can talk later. Right now I want to be with Tempel." She believes citizens should personally witness the horrors of combat to know firsthand what price their freedom. The vast majority of Lunarians agree but only she's privileged to see it real-time.

"Yes, of course. Do you mind if I link to you?" Lazarus asks.

"Not at all, but be warned, I'm going to be fully immersed with Tempel and the others. I expect this will be brutal. It may be more than you can handle," Lindsey said.

Lazarus stiffens, "I'm sure I'll be fine."

With jarring suddenness, he's out on the surface looking through the eyes of Tempel, moving rapidly over the rough terrain in a fashion that doesn't seem quite right. He's in the lead so the others are not in sight. He can hear Tempel breath and see his hands reach out, gripping the lunar surface, propelling himself forward.

Suddenly he realizes what's so strange about the movement. Tempel is bounding across the landscape using all four limbs. Even as this realization hits him, the lieutenant turns his head and glances at his companions, giving Lazarus a glimpse of their unique quadruped motion. Smooth and graceful, it is a hybrid motion somewhere between mountain gorilla and cheetah. Their long slender necks allow them to look forward while sprinting across the land, and the joints in their hips and shoulders move in ways impossible for Lazarus.

Their weapons have rotated up over their backs and point forward well above the tops of their heads. The flexibility of the vacsuits has never been more evident as the spines of these young Lunarians bend and twist in a powerful display of agility and power. They are beautiful to behold as they bound across the landscape in giant leaps.

Lazarus is speechless. His mind struggles to grasp what he's witnessing. Many mystifying occurrences over the past few days now crystallize within his mind. These people are different in ways he's only beginning to understand.

"Lindsey… Please explain what I'm seeing," Lazarus asks with trepidation. This frightens him to his core and threatens to destroy the good feeling he's had since his arrival.

Lindsey sighs and pushes Tempel's video signal into the corner where she can monitor it while she talks. It will take a few moments for them to reach their targets. She can give Lazarus that time. "Tempel and the others are… special."

"What do you mean special?" Lazarus presses.

"They have been given gifts that enhance those given to them by Mother Nature."

"So it's true, they're mutants?" Lazarus asks bluntly.

Lindsey barely suppresses her anger. "Like many other names given to people in the past, the term mutant is unacceptable. If you use it again, you will find out very quickly that your freedom does not extend to insults based in ignorance."

The sharp edge in Lindsey's voice signals Lazarus that he's treading on thin ice.

"I meant no offense... It's incredible. Are they another race?"

"No, not really, but they call themselves Highlanders."

"Are you serious?" Lazarus asks.

"The scientists named them something quite different, but they prefer Highlander and now everybody uses the name," Lindsey said.

Glancing at the small image in the corner of her visor, she sees that Quan Kiai is nearing their assigned positions. "Can we discuss this later?"

"Yes… of course," Lazarus said. He re-links with Lindsey to watch the battle. Questions swirl through his mind but he wasn't going to miss this for anything.

ᴙⱢ

Tempel spots their quarry as they come around a sweeping curve. From over a kilometer away, the thermal emissions of the soldiers highlight them in blazing red along the top of the ridge. They are standing together near a large basalt boulder, the only thing breaking the barren ridge for a long ways. Most are looking down upon the crash site, oblivious to the approaching Lunarians.

In single file, the warriors angle up the steep mountainside. At the top, Tempel, Sam, and Zoey turn and head straight for the group along the crest of the ridge. Angel continues down the other side leading Brice and Karyl towards the south end of the Brotherhood camp. None of the warriors break stride as they sprint across the vertical environment, bounding upward with the same grace and agility they demonstrated on the level.

Across Nell's Valley, Karyl, Alonzo and Tatiana swarm over the ridge almost directly above their primary target, the fighters. They spread out into attack formation as they come. Already on the valley floor, Consuela leads Marcel and Corazon from the opposite direction toward the other end of the camp. None has fired a shot, but that will soon change. The four teams are rapidly converging on the unsuspecting camp.

The upper portion of the frigate contains most of the Brotherhood's long-range communications. Kitajima slowly brings his Moonhawk up until he can just peek over the ridge and see the sensor array through the Gattling's gun sights. Magnified and targeted, he times his attack to coincide with his platoon reaching their initial objectives. An instant before Quan Kiai begin their attack, he opens up. His disrupter vaporizes the ceramic armor in a silent explosion, relentlessly drilling into the ship until the pressurized atmosphere bursts forth.

One of the men on the ridge points down into the valley. To a man, the sentry's all look down, a fatal mistake. Bounding along the top of the ridge like hounds from hell, Tempel, Sam and Zoey spread out and begin firing with an inhuman accuracy.

The Lunarians see only Brotherhood combat vacsuits, heavy with plate armor. The men behind the grotesque battle helmets are simply targets on a shooting range. One, two, three, four, five, six, seven, eight, nine, die before they even know the Lunarians are there, cut down like wheat during harvest.

Blood rises in a gaseous haze that takes on a life of its own. Within moments, the ridge above Nell's Valley is a meat grinder. The tenth sentry manages to turn and the eleventh levels his weapon just before they add their blood to the carnage. The twelfth ducks behind the boulder, extending his life by almost a second.

Tempel shoots him in the head as he leaps over the rock. He leads Sam and Zoey downward into Nell's Valley, leaving the expanding cloud of blood and fluids behind.

Synchronized with Kitajima's first shot, Tatiana, Karyl and Alonzo launch missiles at the fighters now less than a hundred meters away. The deadly little finless darts, less than eight centimeters long and two centimeters in diameter, leap from their shoulder mounted launchers and streak towards their targets. In a blur, they strike the fighters and punch through the thin skin. Like a stick of dynamite in a shoebox, the explosion tears them apart. Neither come close to making it off the ground. Karyl sees a figure crawling away from the wreckage and laces his back with disrupter fire. A reddish brown fog erupts from the wounds.

Consuela, Marcel, and Corazon launch missiles at the two vehicles setting west of the camp. The explosions rip open the tank section of the closest, dumping the fluid inside onto the ground where it immediately begins to boil. The other tanker follows a similar fate and the released liquid forms a thick fog that hangs in the vacuum. It's undoubtedly either hydrazine or aniline, one component in the hypergolic fuel used in magnetoplasma thrusters and high capacity fuel cells. Corazon shoots several men when they emerge from the second vehicle, adding their blood to the ghastly mix.

Brice, Angel and Kipper descend into the valley east of Tempel's position and race towards that end of the camp. Several rovers and an armed Goliath are providing security for that side of the camp while keeping the hypergolic constituents separated. From well away, Angel magnifies her target, firing at the Goliath's forward section, probing for its power pack. A second burst from her laser cannon finds its mark. The vehicle explodes in a huge fireball.

Brice and Kipper sprint down the side of the valley firing as fast as their disrupters can recharge. First one rover, then the other explodes as their hypergolic fuels mix. Soldiers run to get away from the unseen death that has descended upon them. Kipper targets the nearest man, almost cutting him in half as he concentrates all his firepower on the soldier's center of mass. Blood spews grotesquely into the vacuum as his body comes to rest, instantly turning to gas.

Brice hits the second and third rovers in rapid secession as he springs forward, sending more fireballs skyward. The men previously clustered around the vehicles, scatter, seeking cover from the terrain but finding none. The few boulders big enough to offer any security are several hundred meters away along the north side of the valley. Digging in his hands and feet, Brice skids to a stop causing a huge wave of fine lunar regolith to rise around him marking his location. Starting with the man furthest back, one by one he picks off the fleeing soldiers. Their lifeless bodies lie across the landscape like some gruesome dotted line.

Brice remains stationary for too long. A beam slams into his chest missing his heart but slicing through his lung. His blood and other bodily fluids spew into the vacuum. He lives long enough to know he's dying.

"No." Marcel cries out.

"Maintain discipline." Kitajima orders roughly. "Finish the job." Brice had broken the cardinal rule, never stop. It cost him dearly.

The others are aware that Brice is down but they have all been taught the best way to help wounded comrades was to finish the fight and leave the medical issues to others. It's the medico's job to monitor vital signs and initiate treatment as needed. Doc Grady can do nothing to save Brice.

Kipper sends a SuperX missile into a Goliath. It penetrates and explodes, ripping open the high capacity fuel cell. A fraction of a second later, a second much larger explosion splits open the massive four-wheeler, silently sending an intense fireball mushrooming skyward. The force of the blast picks up a nearby rover and flips it on its side. Kipper laces the rover's exposed underbelly with a long burst. Another silent ball of flame rises above the shredded carcass of the vehicle.

Virtually invisible to the Brotherhood, the warriors converge on the camp from all directions. Leaping over and around anything in their path, they deliver a massive dose of death and destruction.

Soaring over the top of a large boulder, Tempel shoots a soldier square in the back killing him instantly. The man flops to the surface like a rag doll, gushing blood. Vacuum rips the blood asunder, adding its bits to the growing gaseous haze gathering over the battlefield like smog over a city.

Sam opens fire on a group of soldiers running away from the carnage, cutting them down like wheat before a scythe. None survive. Switching targets to a nearby rover, she blasts several holes in its hypergolic fuel tanks. A moment later, the fuels mix and silently explode.

From the far side of the flame, two Brotherhood soldiers draw Zoey's attention. Leaping through the dissipating fireball, she shoots each one in the chest as she passes between them in a blur too fast for Earth born human's to handle. A blood-red cloud spews from the two men as they fall to the ground, landing flat on their backs, side by side. She lands beyond the dead soldiers and digs her hands deep into the regolith. Twisting, she coils her legs and pushes off, changing directions in the blink of an eye. Zoey's already homing in on her next target.

A short distance away, Tempel spots a rover picking up speed heading out of the valley. Overtaking the vehicle, he fires into the back of each occupant. For good measure, he puts another burst through the rover's power pack as he passes. The rover hits a boulder and tumbles spewing hypergolic fuels. He doesn't wait to see what happens next.

Marcel attacks the parked convoys from broadside, letting loose a pair of SuperX missiles at the nearest. One missile hits between the balloon tires near the articulation joint, the second hits the main passenger compartment above the front tire. The four-wheeled Goliath explodes. Those inside did not have time to don a vacsuit.

Tatiana leads Karyl and Alonzo past the remains of the pilothouse. They use the wreckage as cover and pop out on the far side with their cannons blazing. The warriors speed and stealth surprise the soldiers gathered there. Before they have time to realize what's happening, the Lunarians annihilate their ranks. They aim for center of mass as they sprint past. Not one of the twenty-two soldiers gets off a shot.

Almost as an afterthought, Tatiana launches a missile through the front view port of the second Goliath. The explosion bounces the big vehicle, splitting the pressure hull and releasing the internal atmosphere in a surge of gases that rises a hundred meters into the sky. She launches a second missile at the lone remaining truck, angled downward this time, aiming for the high-capacity power supply buried in its gut. It explodes violently.

From behind the wreckage of the pilothouse, four Brotherhood soldiers open fire on the dark shadows that just went past.

"Kipper. The freighter." Tatiana calls.

She could have saved her breath. Kipper and Angel are already there. They leap over Evolution's Child and engage the soldiers from above and behind. Focused on Tatiana and the others, they never realize that death has found them until it's too late. The warriors mow them down like ducks on a pond. Angel's only shot on the last soldier was an exposed arm. She didn't hesitate, burning a hole in the forearm right below the elbow. Blood spews forth in a bloody fog. The soldier puts his other hand over the wound but can't slow the rush. He slumps to the ground and vacuum finishes the job.

"Clear." Angel calls out, looking for her next target.

Corazon, Marcel, and Consuela swing around the twisted remains of the fuel tankers and bear down on the frigate. They can see the Goliath parked just beyond it. To their left is a group of non-combatants, probably mechanics or technicians, heading as fast as they can back towards the main camp. On foot, they pose little threat. The warriors can't even detect a weapon on any of them. Corazon swings wide and opens up as soon as he's clear. One, two, three go down and the remaining men stop and raise their arms in surrender. Corazon appreciates them providing such an easy target. Spacing his shots right down the line, he nails all six dead center from over a hundred meters away. Their blood adds to the growing battlefield haze.

Beyond them, three rovers are coming up to speed and heading up the valley away from the battle. Targeting the closest, Consuela's first shot locks up the front drive wheels causing the vehicle to careen into a large basalt outcrop, coming to a sudden and violent stop. She chews up the now stationary target making sure nothing could survive. The other rovers open fire trying vainly to hit something they cannot see.

Like a hunting wolf, Consuela parallels the remaining two rovers. They race over the valley floor at speeds exceeding fifty kilometers per hour. Her first volley misses the lead rover's power pack. She turns her attention to the driver. The rover begins trailing bloody fog then veers off course striking a large boulder, flips on its side, and skids across the lunar surface. One more burst in its exposed underbelly sends the buggy up in a hypergolic ball of flame.

Kitajima hammers at the larger ship, concentrating first on the thrusters then on the weapon turrets. He never sees the rover coming at him. The first beam cut through the Moonhawk and passes between Lazarus and Kitajima about shoulder high. The second beam strikes Kitajima in the right temple. His head explodes.

The Moonhawk dips and loses altitude. It would have crashed if Lindsey hadn't grabbed the virtual controls.

"Oh shit." Lindsey banks and accelerates away from the rover. "Lazarus. Take control of the cannon."

Lazarus is stunned. He is in the middle of a brutal battle in a way he had never imagined possible, Brice is dead, Kitajima is dead, and somehow he must pull himself together and do something he's never done before.

"Lazarus." Lindsey said. "I'm not Kitajima. I can't fly and fight at the same time."

"How?" Lazarus stutters.

Lindsey transfers the cannon function to his visor. "Just look at what you want to hit and press this icon."

She swings the ship around and heads back. The rover was trading shots with Consuela and didn't see the approaching Moonhawk. Lazarus locks his gaze on it and fires. The beam passes through the roll cage without touching anything.

"Magnify," Lindsey orders.

Lazarus magnifies and fires again and again and again. He turns the driver into a reddish brown fog. The rover skids to a stop.

"That's it. Keep firing." Lindsey said.

The rover explodes a moment later, its fuel tanks punctured.

"Nice shooting." Consuela said.

Lindsey had chased the rover out onto the valley floor and the Brotherhood frigate still had some fight left in it. Beams slash through the Moonhawk and several hit Kitajima again. Inside the ship is a bloody haze that clings to everything it touches.

Lazarus turns his gaze on the frigate and continues to fire as fast as the cannon can reenergize. He finishes the job Kitajima started, obliterating the last of the frigates gun turrets. He didn't stop. He pumps shot after shot into the sitting target. Explosions rock it and escaping air hangs over the doomed ship.

"Consuela, take command of Moonhawk One," Tempel orders.

Showing tremendous strength, Consuela digs into the soft regolith making a sharp turn towards the frigate. The dust of her passage settles slowly behind her.

Marcel and Corazon launch missiles at the warship as they pass, not waiting around to see the results. To their left, two rovers are sprinting away from the camp. Firing from over two hundred meters away, their disrupters hit within centimeters of their target, ripping at the vehicles underbelly, probing relentlessly for the power pack. The hypergolic fluids react in a towering ball of flame, ripping the rover apart. Its companion vehicle meets the same fate a second later, exploding with a force that sends one of its balloon tires bouncing wildly across the valley floor.

Sam sprints down the debris field. To her right she spots motion along the ground as a soldier crawls away. A burst along his spine stops all movement. Swinging around the wreckage of the pilothouse, Sam launches a missile at the frigate. It hits the fuselage near a landing strut and rips apart the superstructure. The frigate collapses, its remaining landing struts partially holding it up. Gases gush from gaping holes in its skin.

The last three rovers speed towards the north end of the valley away from the camp, running for their lives. Hidden behind the frigate for most of their sprint, they are a kilometer away before anyone notices them, and only then because the gunner in the lead rover cannot resist taking a pot shot at a shadow.

Marcel spots the three vehicles racing up the valley after his targeting system lets him know he's under fire. Hitting a fast moving rover at that distance is tricky, even for Marcel. Leaping in pursuit, he closes the gap. At the top of a leap, he fires and the rover last in line erupts in flame, fails to make a turn and slams into a large basalt outcropping. The second rover detonates a moment later. Trailing a cloud of bloody gases, the final rover crests a ridge and disappears, the only vehicle to survive

Nell's Valley.

"Let them go." Tempel orders, pulling Marcel up short. "Someone should live to tell of what happened here today."

The attack lasted less than two minutes. A fog of death hangs thick over the valley. It'll take days for the cloud to disperse and years before their sensors can't detect it forensically.

"Hack, get in here. Lindsey, land Moonhawk Two per the plan. Hack, help her. Kipper, you and Doc Grady take care of Brice and the Captain," Tempel takes command. "Sam, you're with me."

"Aye," she said.

Lindsey lands just beyond the wreckage of the pilothouse. Sam crawls into the hole. If the bomb isn't already exposed, they will need to keep the excavator digging until it was. That's her job.

Lazarus emerges from the Moonhawk, "What can I do to help?"

"It's still several meters to the crate," Sam replies. "But this is a Hodgkin's excavator assembled right here on Luna. It'll make short work of it."

"Good, then let's get started," Lazarus said.

"You stay out of the way," Sam said to his chagrin.

"Quan Kiai, listen up," Tempel said. "We have two minutes of digging and another two to get the crate loaded. You have that long to collect intelligence. Follow the plan, Angel and Alonzo take the frigate, Consuela and Corazon the shelter, Tatiana, Karyl and Zoey poke around what's left of the Goliaths. You know what you're looking for. Let's move out."

Approaching the heavily damaged frigate, Angel and Alonzo can see the main airlock is beyond use. The two warriors climb the side of the ship heading towards a big hole. The Lunarians peer inside then crawl through. The frigate has no power forcing their visors to increase sensitivity in the low-light-level sensors.

The floor tilts at a crazy angle. Everything loose slid downhill when the ship tipped over and is in one big pile at the bottom.

"This must have been living quarters. Come on. Let's see where this leads." Alonzo scampers up the angled floor heading for an open door above them. He pulls himself through the doorway into the next room.

Angel follows, leaping through the doorway without touching the sides. She lands on all fours. The room is thick with gases. The large quantities of blood and urine testify that more than one person died here. That isn't their concern right now. This isn't a forensic mission. They're looking for loot in the form of knowledge.

Along the side of the room is a passage leading upward. Angel takes it, emerging on what is obviously the ships control room. Bodies lie against one wall in a tangled heap of arms and legs. From the looks of things, no one had vacsuits on at the time of the attack. They paid dearly for their carelessness.

Banks of electronic equipment line the walls. Alonzo stops at a large floor-to-ceiling rack, running his hand down the front, analyzing the markings on each piece of equipment.

"Here. This is the AI. It's marked in Arabic, Chinese, and English. They must have bought it on the open market." Alonzo said.

"Get it and let's go. We don't have all day." Angel flares, clinging to the edge of a console near what must have been the command chair. Blood smears one armrest and two holes are neatly punched in its back. She finds a small book tucked in a pocket and recognizes it as the Captains personal log, a practice the Brotherhood continues from the earlier days of sea faring ships.

Alonzo looks around in panic, "Shit. I don't have a screwdriver."

Angel smiles as she slips the book into a pocket of her ghost suit. She scrambles past Alonzo, finds a good angle, and opens up with her disrupter on the metal framework of the rack, deftly cutting the AI out with surgical skill.

Alonzo meekly assists in cutting the fiber-optic cabling from the back of the device as Angel pulls it free from the rack. She then moves behind Alonzo and secures the device to the warriors back.

Leaping from the frigate, the Lunarians sprint back to the Moonhawk, storing their booty in the cargo hold.

"Angel, Alonzo… get over here and lend a hand." Sam calls.

Scrambling around the wreck, they dig in their heels and pull mightily at the ropes. The emerging crate threatens to buckle under the strength of the Highlanders.

"Easy." Sam calls out. "The auto-detonate is still active."

Lazarus and Sam frantically scoop away the regolith that had gathered in front of the crate. The warriors grunt and pull, and grunt some more, muscling it out of the narrow passage. They finally get it on the surface.

"Lindsey, once this is secured in the hold, I want you to disarm the booby trap. But be careful. Don't assume it's identical to the others."

"Aye," Lindsey said.

Angel, Sam, Alonzo and Consuela place slings under the crate and carry it the final few meters, depositing it in the transport.

"Let's move it people," Tempel broadcast, standing at the bottom of the ramp, hands on his hips, looking out across the battlefield. They're all back except for Tatiana. "Tatiana, report." He spots her emerging from the remains of a Goliath. She's loaded down, her backpack full and the pockets and pouches of her ghost suit bulge with loot.

A beam from somewhere high overhead vaporizes the surface in front of her. Tatiana leaps sideways and sprints across the lunar surface back to the Moonhawk.

Tatiana replies. "I found some very interesting documents."

"Show me later. We need to get out of here… now." Tempel said. The Brotherhoods battlestation in Lagrange One is joining the fight.

The warriors silently lay Captain Osaka alongside Brice, Lei, and Karl. The Moonhawks rise and disappear into the lunar night.

Epilogue

Major General Arif replays the battle for the tenth time. It's worse than he had feared. The Djinn had technology that made them virtually impossible to see.

His people had extrapolated from the various paths of destruction that there was at least forty Djinn involved in the attack. The battle had lasted for a hundred-eleven seconds and eighty-seven of his men were dead.

One Djinn casualty. One. **Pure madness.**

The sheer speed and efficiency of the Lunarian's attack chills him to the bone. His soldiers will be hard-pressed to match it. The vid showing them killing those men trying to surrender will make good Earthnet news later, but for now, it shakes him to his core.

Major General Arif immediately designates all vid reports of the battle Top Secret Prohibited and seals the records. He can't risk this going viral among his troops.

No, that wouldn't do at all.

Some Things About Chuck

Autobiography

Let me tell you just a little about myself. My folks were divorced before I was three back when divorce was unheard of. Guess they just couldn't take my incessant howling. No matter. They both loved me and that was all I really cared about at that age. I grew up bouncing between Colorado and Southern California and loving every minute of it. By the time I started high school, I had visited every state west of the Mississippi.

Speaking of high school, mine was in a small town on the Mojave Desert. Counting the occasional tourist, Boron topped out at about 5000 souls, but it wasn't boring. The main part of the town is nestled at the feet of a high-desert volcano-looking mountain with a rocket engine test facility built into its summit. Edwards Air Force Base is just on the other side of it from Boron. You could always tell who was new in town; they flinched every time a sonic boom rattled the windows. The mountain we simply called the Rocket Site and ignored the loud noises. They tested the Saturn 5 engines at the Rocket Site, the ones that took our boys to the moon. Once in a while they would fire them up at night. What a sight. What a noise. Those babies would shake the world in a way impossible to describe. It's something that must be felt and then you will never forget it.

Long story short, after four years in the army mostly in Baumholder, Germany, I went to college and earned a BS in Engineering Mechanics-Aerospace from the University of Wisconsin-Madison and a Masters in Materials Science from Arizona State University. For a while I worked at Space Data/Orbital Sciences Corporation designing, building, and launching rockets and high altitude weather balloons. I launched rockets from Mexican, Canadian, and American soil. My sounding rockets even launched from the deck of a French frigate. Later, I was the Quality Assurance Manager for Hybrid Design Associates in Tempe. HDA is a small manufacturing company that specializes in harsh-environment electronic assemblies. Among a host of other customers, we built electronic boards for the oil logging industry, Halliburton, Baker Atlas, Pathfinder, etc.

A couple decades ago I was lucky enough to marry the most wonderful woman in the world. We have three kids and six grand-kids. I run a small publishing company, Writers Cramp Publishing, and write under my full name, Charles Lee Lesher. My debut novel, Evolution's Child, was selected as 2007's Best of the Moon Fiction by the Lunar Library. You can still buy it, but now it is part of the Republic of Luna series. Evolution's Child has morphed into two Kindle novels, *Evolution's Child - Earthman* and *Evolution's Child - Lunarian*. I know, its weird but what can I say. The creative process is not always as neat as we would like. The third book, *Evolution's Child - Thread,* makes this a trilogy. You can also buy all three novels in one big bathroom reader, Shadow on the Moon is 500 pages of science fiction excitement.

I used the research obtained writing the Republic of Luna series to write a nonfiction titled *Out of the Cradle* on sale as a conventional hardcover, a gorgeous Kindle Fire, and now as a Full Color 8.5 x 11 Paperback. The first half of the book will bum you out but the second half will lift you up giving hope to our future. The world is changing and we had better be ready. The biggest change will be energy. Electricity is a key component holding our technological civilization together. What happens when we finally run out of oil and the coal is gone? Don't sweet it. There is an answer and nuclear is not involved, at least, not in your backyard. Buy my book and see how we are doing the impossible.

My latest book is a western set in the Verde Valley before Arizona was a state. The story takes place in the Arizona Territory at a time when the only law enforcement outside the capital city of Prescott was a few men wearing a star. When one of them goes bad, all hell breaks loose.

Chuck's Other Books

Bad Day on the Verde

WESTERN FICTION

Lying awake on the floor, Tom cried out and made a weak play for his Winchester. He was stopped abruptly by the butt of Kingsley's heavy shotgun. Tom slumped back, dazed and bleeding. Kingsley relieved Tom of the rifle.

"I could of killed you, but I didn't. But I will if you give me any trouble." Kingsley gave Tom a real close look at the gaping muzzles of the Baker 10 gauge.

Kingsley rolled Tom onto his stomach tying his hands behind his back, relishing the moans this caused. He pulled Tom's boots off throwing them across the small cabin. Standing, he lashed out and kicked the man savagely in the ass. "Get the hell up, boy."

Bad Day is a western story of violence and brutality, of sudden frontier justice, but also of courage and enduring love. The story takes place in the Arizona Territory at a time when the only law enforcement outside the capital city of Prescott was a few men wearing a star. When one of them goes bad, all hell breaks loose..

ISBN 978-1-938586-72-9 Paperback
ISBN 978-1-938586-73-6 eBook

Shadow on the Moon

SCIENCE FICTION

The Republic of Luna is humanities first extraterrestrial nation. Science, genetics and a humanistic society mark it as a target for the powerful Islamic Brotherhood, a global empire with billions of believers. Luna is a world created by pioneers whose only religion is the humane treatment of one another in their common struggle to survive the ultimate hostile environment, space. The heroes that conquered the moon must now defend it.

Shadow on the Moon combines *Evolution's Child - Earthman, Evolution's Child - Lunarian, Evolution's Child - Thread*, and *Science of the Republic* into one 500 page Anniversary Print Edition.

ISBN: 978-0-977723-56-0 Paperback

Aldrin Station - Rise of Luna

Aldrin Station is a collection of short stories illuminating Lunarian history from the dawn of mankind to its expansion into space and colonizing the moon. These are stories of the families and individuals that play a role in the Republic of Luna.

ISBN 978-1-938586-00-2 eBook

Evolution's Child - Earthman

SCIENCE FICTION

Book One: Lazarus Sheffield is a man without a planet by the time he meets Lindsey on his way to Heaven's Gate Space Station. Lindsey quickly determines that the nervous guy sitting next to her is a high ranking government official on the run from one of history's most repressive governments, the totalitarian theocracy otherwise known as the North American Federation. She decides to help him and introduces Lazarus to some of Luna's finest citizens. So begins Book One of Shadow on the Moon.

ISBN 978-1-938586-06-4 Paperback
ISBN 978-1-938586-01-9 eBook

Evolution's Child - Lunarian

SCIENCE FICTION

Book Two: Tempel Dugan leads a group of Lunarians against impossible odds. They call themselves Quan Kiai. These young warriors, and a few more like them, are all that stands between the Republic of Luna and total annihilation but things are not always as they seem.

ISBN 978-1-938586-07-1 Paperback
ISBN 978-1-938586-02-6 eBook

Evolution's Child - Thread

SCIENCE FICTION

Book Three: The Republic of Luna is teetering at the point of collapse when the Lunarian General Council commits their last hope. They send Quan Kaia and the remaining Lunarian warriors against the Brotherhood. Fight or die. They fight in their great underground cities, they fight cross the surface of the moon, and they fight in orbital space. Earth and Luna become locked in humanities first interplanetary war, the Shadow War.

ISBN 978-1-938586-08-8 Paperback
ISBN 978-1-938586-03-3 eBook

Science of the Republic

A collection of articles, maps, and tables that help the reader understand the science and technology of the Republic.

ISBN 978-1-938586-04-0 eBook

Out of the Cradle

SCIENCE FACT

Where will we get our electricity when the oil and coal are gone? Why should I care? Abundant cheap electricity a key element in getting and maintaining high human living standards around the globe. Stated another way, electricity is the foundation of modern technology. Without it, we go back to sailing ships and the horse. Out the Cradle summarizes the major issues facing the world today and lays out a solution to our global energy needs.

ISBN: 978-0-983750-64-2 Hard Cover
ISBN: 978-0-983750-68-0 eBook

Charles Lee Lesher

8.5 x 11 Color Version
ISBN: 978-1-938586-71-2 Paperback

Writers Cramp Publishing

http://www.writerscramp.us
editor@writerscramp.us
Amazon, Barnes&Noble, Google, Espresso